Also available in the Guys Read Library of Great Reading

GUYS READ

OTHER WORLDS

GUYS READ

OTHER WORLDS

EDITED AND WITH AN INTRODUCTION BY
JON SCIESZKA

STORIES BY

**TOM ANGLEBERGER, RAY BRADBURY,
SHANNON HALE, D. J. MacHALE,
ERIC NYLUND, KENNETH OPPEL,
RICK RIORDAN, NEAL SHUSTERMAN,
REBECCA STEAD, AND SHAUN TAN**

WITH ILLUSTRATIONS BY
GREG RUTH

WALDEN POND PRESS
An Imprint of HarperCollinsPublishers

Walden Pond Press is an imprint of HarperCollins Publishers.
Walden Pond Press and the skipping stone logo are trademarks and registered
trademarks of Walden Media, LLC.

ISBN 978-0-06-196380-3 (trade bdg.) — ISBN 978-0-06-196379-7 (pbk.)

Typography by Joel Tippie
13 14 15 16 17 LP/RRDH 10 9 8 7 6 5 4 3 2 1
❖
First Edition

CONTENTS

BEFORE WE BEGIN . . .

What would happen if invading warlords from another planet landed on your school's basketball court?

Or what if you took your older brother's armor and ran away from home and the only way you could feed yourself was to pretend you were a tough and maybe magically powerful bouncer at a village tavern?

Or what if smart robot shoes joined together to revolt against their human masters?

You would be in the middle of some great science fiction and fantasy. That's what.

All fiction and storytelling is answering that "What if . . . ?" question. But science fiction and fantasy go a step further: They bend the rules of reality. They get to imagine the "What if?" in completely other worlds.

And that is why good science fiction and fantasy stories can be so mind-expandingly fun.

The first science fiction stories I ever read were written by a guy named Ray Bradbury. They were in a book titled *The Illustrated Man*. In it, the tattoos on this guy's body came to life and told stories about an evil house, a Martian soldier, astronauts stranded on Venus, a time travel agency, and a mess of other freaky happenings.

Ray Bradbury died in 2012. And I'm sorry I never got to meet him. Because I wanted to thank him for writing those stories that got me started reading science fiction and fantasy by Isaac Asimov, Arthur C. Clarke, L. Sprague de Camp, Edgar Rice Burroughs, Philip K. Dick, J. R. R. Tolkien, Terry Pratchett, Jules Verne, H. P. Lovecraft, Robert Heinlein, and a mess of others.

Now there are hundreds of amazing new science fiction and fantasy writers. Just look on the back cover of this book. We've got a bunch of the best for you. A nice mix of superstar writers you already know and some surprising writers you will be glad to meet.

We also have one very special addition to this volume. We have a story of Mr. Bradbury's called "Frost and Fire." A tribute to the guy who inspired me, and so many other readers and writers.

Thank you, Ray Bradbury.

Thank you, science fiction and fantasy writers and creators of other worlds.

Jon Scieszka

GUYS READ

OTHER WORLDS

PERCY JACKSON AND THE SINGER OF APOLLO
BY RICK RIORDAN

I know what you're going to ask.

"Percy Jackson, why are you hanging from a Times Square billboard without your pants on, about to fall to your death?"

Good question. You can blame Apollo, god of music, archery, and poetry—also the god of making me do stupid quests.

This particular disaster started when I brought my friend Grover some aluminum cans for his birthday.

Perhaps I should mention . . . I'm a demigod. My dad, Poseidon, is the lord of the sea, which sounds cool, I guess, but mostly it means my life is filled with monster attacks and annoying Greek gods who tend to pop up on the subway or in the middle of math class or when I'm taking a shower. (Long story. Don't ask.)

I figured maybe I'd get a day off from the craziness for Grover's birthday, but of course I was wrong.

Grover and his girlfriend, Juniper, were spending the day in Prospect Park in Brooklyn, doing naturey stuff like dancing with the local tree nymphs and serenading the squirrels. Grover's a satyr. That's his idea of fun.

Juniper seemed to be having an especially good time. While Grover and I sat on the bench together, she frolicked across Long Meadow with the other nature spirits, her chlorophyll-tinted eyes glinting in the sunlight. Since she was a dryad, Juniper's life source was tied to a juniper bush back on Long Island, but Grover explained that she could take short trips away from home as long as she kept a handful of fresh juniper berries in her pockets. I didn't want to ask what would happen if the berries got accidentally smashed.

Anyway, we hung out for a while, talking and enjoying the nice weather. I gave Grover his aluminum cans, which may sound like a lame gift, but that's his favorite snack.

He happily munched on the cans while the nymphs

started discussing what party games we should play. Grover pulled a blindfold out of his pocket and suggested Pin the Tail on the Human, which made me kind of nervous since I was the only human.

Then, without warning, the sunlight brightened. The air turned uncomfortably hot. Twenty feet away, the grass hissed and a cloud of steam whooshed up like somebody opened a big pressing machine at a Laundromat. The steam cleared, and standing in front of us was the god Apollo.

Gods can look like anything they want, but Apollo always seemed to go for that I-just-auditioned-for-a-boy-band look. Today he was rocking pencil-thin jeans, a white muscle shirt, and gilded Ray-Ban sunglasses. His wavy blond hair glistened with product. When he smiled the dryads squealed and giggled.

"Oh, no . . ." Grover murmured. "This can't be good."

"Percy Jackson!" Apollo beamed at me. "And, um, your goat friend—"

"His name is Grover," I said. "And we're kind of off duty, Lord Apollo. It's Grover's birthday."

"Happy birthday!" Apollo said. "I'm so glad you're taking the day off. That means you two have time to help me with a small problem!"

Naturally, the problem wasn't small.

Apollo led Grover and me away from the party so we could talk in private. Juniper didn't want to let Grover go, but she couldn't argue with a god. Grover promised to come back safely. I hoped it was a promise he'd be able to keep.

When we got to the edge of the woods, Apollo faced us. "Allow me to introduce the chryseae celedones."

The god snapped his fingers. More steam erupted from the ground and three golden women appeared in front of us. When I say golden, I mean they were literally gold. Their metallic skin glittered. Their sleeveless gowns were made from enough gilded fabric to finance a bailout. Their golden hair was braided and piled on top of their heads in a sort of classical beehive hairdo. They were uniformly beautiful, and uniformly terrifying.

I'd seen living statues—automatons—many times before. Beautiful or not, they almost always tried to kill me.

"Uh . . ." I took a step back. "What did you say these were? Krissy Kelly something?"

"Chryseae celedones," Apollo said. "Golden singers. They're my backup band!"

I glanced at Grover, wondering if this was some kind of joke.

Grover wasn't laughing. His mouth hung open in amazement, as if the golden ladies were the largest, tastiest aluminum cans he'd ever seen. "I—I didn't think they were real!"

Apollo smiled. "Well, it's been a few centuries since I brought them out. If they perform too often, you know, their novelty wears off. They used to live at my temple in Delphi. Man, they could rock that place. Now I only use them for special occasions."

Grover got teary-eyed. "You brought them out for my birthday?"

Apollo laughed. "No, fool! I've got a concert tonight on Mount Olympus. Everyone is going to be there! The Nine Muses are opening, and I'm performing a mix of old favorites and new material. I mean, it's not like I need the celedones. My solo career has been great. But people will expect to hear some of my classic hits with the girls: 'Daphne on My Mind,' 'Stairway to Olympus,' 'Sweet Home Atlantis.' It's going to be awesome!"

I tried not to look nauseous. I'd heard Apollo's poetry before, and if his music was even half that bad, this concert was going to blow harder than Aeolus the wind god.

"Great," I said half-heartedly. "So what's the problem?"

Apollo's smile faded. "Listen."

He turned to his golden singers and raised his hands like a conductor. On cue, they sang in harmony: "Laaaa!"

It was only one chord, but it filled me with bliss. I suddenly couldn't remember where I was or what I was doing. If the golden singers had decided to tear me to pieces at that moment, I wouldn't have resisted, as long as they kept singing. Nothing mattered to me, except the sound.

Then the golden girls went silent. The feeling passed. Their faces returned to beautiful, impassive metal.

"That . . ." I swallowed. "That was amazing."

"Amazing?" Apollo wrinkled his nose. "There are only three of them! Their harmonies sound empty. I can't perform without the full quartet."

Grover was weeping with joy. "They're so beautiful. They're perfect!"

I was kind of glad Juniper wasn't within earshot, since she's the jealous type.

Apollo crossed his tan arms. "They're not perfect, Mr. Satyr. I need all four or the concert will be ruined. Unfortunately, my fourth celedon went rogue this morning. I can't find her anywhere."

I looked at the three golden automatons, staring at Apollo, quietly waiting for orders. "Uh . . . how does a backup singer go rogue?"

Apollo made another conductor wave, and the singers sighed in three-part harmony. The sound was so mournful my heart sank into my gut. At that moment, I felt sure I'd never be happy again. Then, just as quickly, the feeling dissipated.

"They're out of warranty," the god explained. "Hephaestus made them for me back in the old days, and they worked fine . . . until the day after their two-thousand-year warranty expired. Then, naturally, WHAM! The fourth one goes haywire and runs off to the big city." He gestured in the general direction of Manhattan. "Of course I tried to complain to Hephaestus, but he's all, 'Well, did you have my Protection Plus package?' And I'm like, 'I didn't want your stupid extended warranty!' And he acts as if it's my fault the celedon broke, and says if I'd bought the Plus package, I could've had a dedicated service hotline, but—"

"Whoa, whoa, whoa." I interrupted. I really didn't want to get in the middle of a god-versus-god argument. I'd been there too many times. "So if you know that your celedon is in the city, why can't you just look for her yourself?"

"I don't have time! I have to practice. I have to write a set list and do a sound check! Besides, this is what heroes are for."

"Running the gods' errands," I muttered.

"Exactly." Apollo spread his hands. "I assume the missing celedon is roaming the Theater District, looking for a suitable place to audition. Celedones have the usual starlet dreams—being discovered, headlining a Broadway musical, that sort of thing. Most of the time I can keep their ambitions under control. I mean I can't have them upstaging me, can I? But I'm sure without me around she thinks she's the next Katy Perry. You two need to get her before she causes any problems. And hurry! The concert is tonight and Manhattan is a large island."

Grover tugged his goatee. "So . . . you want us to find her while you do sound checks?"

"Think of it as a favor," Apollo said. "Not just for me, but for all those mortals in Manhattan."

"Oh." Grover's voice got very small. "Oh, no . . ."

"What?" I demanded. "What oh, no?"

Years ago, Grover created a magic empathy link between us (another long story) and we could sense each other's emotions. It wasn't exactly mind reading, but I could tell he was terrified.

"Percy," he said, "if that celedon starts singing in public, in the middle of afternoon rush hour—"

"She'll cause no end of havoc," Apollo said. "She might

sing a love song, or a lullaby, or a patriotic war tune, and whatever the mortals hear . . ."

I shuddered. One sigh from the golden girls had plunged me into despair, even with Apollo controlling their power. I imagined a rogue celedon busting into song in a crowded city—putting people to sleep, or making them fall in love, or urging them to fight.

"She has to be stopped," I agreed. "But why us?"

"I like you!" Apollo grinned. "You've faced the Sirens before. This isn't too different. Just put some wax in your ears. Besides, your friend Grover here is a satyr. He has nat-ural resistance to magical music. Plus he can play the lyre."

"What lyre?" I asked.

Apollo snapped his fingers. Suddenly Grover was hold-ing the weirdest musical instrument I'd ever seen. The base was a hollowed-out tortoise shell, which made me feel really bad for the tortoise. Two polished wooden arms stuck out one side like a bull's horns, with a bar across the top and seven strings stretching from the bar to the base of the shell. It looked like a combination harp, banjo, and dead turtle.

"Oh!" Grover almost dropped the lyre. "I couldn't! This is your—"

"Yes," Apollo agreed cheerfully. "That's my own personal

lyre. Of course if you damage it, I'll incinerate you, but I'm sure you'll be careful! You can play the lyre, can't you?"

"Um . . ." Grover plucked a few notes that sounded like a funeral dirge.

"Keep practicing," Apollo said. "You'll need the lyre's magic to capture the celedon. Have Percy distract her while you play."

"Distract her," I repeated.

This quest was sounding worse and worse. I didn't see how a tortoiseshell harp could defeat a golden automaton, but Apollo clapped me on the shoulder like everything was settled.

"Excellent!" he said. "I'll meet you at the Empire State Building at sunset. Bring me the celedon. One way or another I'll persuade Hephaestus to fix her. Just don't be late! I can't keep my audience waiting. And remember, not a scratch on that lyre."

Then the sun god and his golden backup singers disappeared in a cloud of steam.

"Happy birthday to me," Grover whimpered, and plucked a sour note on the lyre.

We caught the subway to Times Square. We figured that would be a good place to start looking. It was in the middle of the Theater District and full of weird street performers and about a billion tourists, so it was the natural place for a golden diva to get some attention for herself.

Grover hadn't bothered disguising himself. His white T-shirt read: What Would Pan Do? The tips of his horns stuck out from his curly hair. Usually he wore jeans over his shaggy legs and specially fitted shoes over his hooves, but today from the waist down he was au naturel goat.

I doubted it would matter. Most mortals couldn't see through the Mist, which hid the true appearance of monsters. Even without Grover's normal disguise, people would have to look really closely to notice he was a satyr, and even then they probably wouldn't bat an eye. This was New York, after all.

As we pushed through the crowd, I kept searching for the glint of gold, hoping to spot the rogue celedon, but the square was packed as usual. A guy wearing only his underwear and a guitar was having his picture taken with some tourists. Cops hung out on the street corners, looking bored. At Broadway and West Forty-Ninth, the intersection was blocked and a crew of roadies was setting up some sort of stage. Preachers, ticket scalpers, and hawkers shouted over each other, trying to get attention. Music blasted from dozens of loudspeakers, but I didn't hear any magical singing.

Grover had given me a ball of warm wax to stuff in

my ears whenever necessary. He said he always kept some handy, like chewing gum, which didn't make me eager to use it.

He bumped into a pretzel vendor's cart and lurched back, hugging Apollo's lyre protectively.

"You know how to use that thing?" I asked. "I mean, what kind of magic does it do?"

Grover's eyes widened. "You don't know? Apollo built the walls of Troy just by playing this lyre. With the right song, it can create almost anything!"

"Like a cage for the celedon?" I asked.

"Uh . . . yeah!"

He didn't sound too confident, and I wasn't sure I wanted him playing Guitar Hero with a godly tortoise banjo. Sure, Grover could do some magic with his reed pipes. On a good day, he could make plants grow and tangle his enemies. On a bad day, he could only remember Justin Bieber songs, which didn't do anything except give me a headache.

I tried to think of a plan. I wished my girlfriend, Annabeth, was here. She was more of the planning type. Unfortunately, she was off in San Francisco visiting her dad.

Grover grabbed my arm. "There."

I followed his gaze. Across the square, at the outdoor stage, workers scurried around, installing lights on the scaffolding, setting up microphone stands, and plugging in giant speakers. Probably they were prepping for a Broadway musical preview or something.

Then I saw her—a golden lady making her way toward the platform. She climbed over the police barricades that cordoned off the intersection, squeezed between workers who completely ignored her, and headed for the steps, stage right. She glanced at the crowd in Times Square and smiled, as if imagining their wild applause. Then she headed for the center microphone.

"Oh, gods!" Grover yelped. "If that sound system is on . . ."

I stuffed wax in my ears as we ran for the stage.

Fighting automatons is bad enough. Fighting one in a crowd of mortals is a recipe for disaster. I didn't want to worry about the mortals' safety and mine and figure out how to capture the celedon. I needed a way to evacuate Times Square without causing a stampede.

As we wove through the crowd, I grabbed the nearest cop by the shoulder.

"Hey!" I told him. "Presidential motorcade coming! You guys better clear the streets!"

I pointed down Seventh Avenue. Of course there was no

motorcade, but I did my best to imagine one.

See, some demigods can actually control the Mist. They can make people see what they want them to see. I wasn't very good at it, but it was worth a shot. Presidential visits are common enough, with the United Nations in town and all, so I figured the cop might buy it.

Apparently he did. He glanced toward my imaginary line of limos, made a disgusted face, and said something into his two-way radio. With the wax in my ears, I couldn't hear what, but all the other cops in the square started herding the crowd toward the side streets.

Unfortunately, the celedon had reached center stage.

We were still fifty feet away when she grabbed the mike and tapped it. BOOM, BOOM, BOOM echoed through the streets.

"Grover," I yelled, "you'd better start playing that lyre."

If he responded, I didn't hear it. I sprinted for the stage. The workers were too busy arguing with the cops to try stopping me. I bounded up the steps, pulled my pen from my pocket, and uncapped it. My sword, Riptide, sprang into existence, though I wasn't sure it would help me. Apollo wouldn't be happy with me if I decapitated his backup singer.

I was twenty feet from the celedon when a lot of things happened at once.

The golden singer belted out a note so powerful I could hear it through the wax plugs. Her voice was heartbreakingly sad, filled with longing. Even muffled through the wax, it made me want to break down and cry—which is what several thousand people around Times Square did. Cars stopped. Police and tourists fell to their knees, weeping, hugging each other in consolation.

Then I became aware of a different sound—Grover, frantically strumming his lyre. I couldn't exactly hear it, but I could feel the tremor of magic rippling through the air, shaking the stage under my feet. Thanks to the empathy link, I caught flashes of Grover's thoughts. He was singing about walls, trying to summon a box around the celedon.

The good news: It sort of worked. A brick wall erupted from the stage between me and the celedon, knocking over the mike stand and interrupting her song. The bad news: By the time I figured out what was going on, I couldn't stop my momentum. I ran straight into the wall, which wasn't mortared, so I promptly collapsed on top of the celedon along with about a thousand bricks.

My eyes watered. My nose felt broken. Before I could regain my bearings, the celedon struggled out of the pile of bricks and pushed me off. She raised her arms in triumph as if the whole thing had been a planned stunt.

She sang, "Ta-daaaaah!"

She was no longer amplified, but her voice carried. The mortals stopped sobbing and rose to their feet, clapping and cheering for the celedon.

"Grover!" I yelled, not sure if he could hear me. "Play something else!"

I picked up my sword and struggled to my feet. I tackled the golden lady, but it was like tackling a lamppost. She ignored me and launched into song.

As I wrestled her, trying to pull her off balance, the temperature onstage began to rise. The celedon's lyrics were in Ancient Greek, but I caught a few of the words: Apollo, sunlight, golden fire. It was some kind of ode to the god. Her metal skin grew hot. I smelled something burning and realized it was my shirt.

I stumbled away from her, my clothes smoldering. The wax had melted out of my ears so I could hear her song clearly. All around Times Square, people started dropping from the heat.

Over at the barricades, Grover played wildly on the lyre, but he was too anxious to focus. Random bricks fell from the sky. One of the monitor speakers on stage morphed into a chicken. A plate of enchiladas appeared at the celedon's feet.

"Not helpful!" I shouted through the pain of the rising heat. "Sing about cages! Or gags!"

The air felt like a blast furnace. If the celedon kept this up, Midtown would burst into flames. I couldn't afford to play nice anymore. As the celedon started her next verse, I lunged at her with my sword.

She lurched away with surprising speed. The tip of my blade missed her face by an inch. I'd managed to stop her singing, and she was not happy about it. She glared at me with outrage, then focused on my blade. Fear flickered across her metallic face. Most magical beings knew enough to respect Celestial bronze, since it could vaporize them on contact.

"Surrender and I won't hurt you," I said. "We just want to take you back to Apollo."

She spread her arms. I was afraid she was going to sing again, but instead the celedon changed form. Her arms grew into golden feathery wings. Her face elongated, growing a beak. Her body shrank until I was staring at a plump metal bird about the size of a quail. Before I could react, the celedon launched herself in the air and flew straight for the top of the nearest building.

Grover stumbled onto the stage next to me. All across Times Square, the mortals who had collapsed from the heat were starting to recover. The pavement still steamed. Police started shouting orders, making a serious effort now to clear the area. Nobody paid us any attention.

I watched the golden bird spiral up until she disappeared over the highest billboard on the Times Tower. You've probably seen the building in pictures: the tall skinny one that's stacked with glowing advertisements and Jumbo-tron screens.

To be completely honest, I didn't feel so great. I had hot wax melting out of my ears. I'd been charbroiled medium rare. My face felt like it had just been rammed into a brick wall . . . because it had. I had the coppery taste of blood in my mouth, and I was really starting to hate music. And quails.

I turned to Grover. "Did you know she could morph into a bird?"

"Uh, yeah . . . But I kind of forgot."

"Great." I nudged the enchilada plate at my feet. "Could you try to summon something more helpful next time?"

"Sorry," he murmured. "I get hungry when I get nervous. So what do we do now?"

I stared up at the top of the Times Tower. "The golden girl wins round one. Time for round two."

∗   ∗   ∗

You're probably wondering why I didn't put more wax in my ears. For one thing, I didn't have any. For another thing, wax melting out of my ears hurts. And maybe part of me was thinking: Hey, I'm a demigod. This time I'm prepared. I can face the music, literally.

Grover assured me he had the lyre figured out. No more enchiladas or bricks falling from the sky. I just had to find the celedon, catch her by surprise, and distract her by . . . well, I hadn't figured out that part yet.

We took the elevator to the top floor and found stairs to the roof. I wished I could fly, but that wasn't one of my powers, and my pegasus friend Blackjack hadn't been answering my calls for help lately. (He gets a little distracted in the springtime when he's searching the skies for cute lady pegasi.)

Once we made it to the roof, the celedon was easy to find. She was in human form, standing at the edge of the building with her arms spread, serenading Times Square with her own rendition of "New York, New York."

I really hate that song. I don't know anybody who's actually from New York who doesn't hate that song, but hearing her sing it made me hate it a whole lot more.

Anyway, she had her back to us, so we had an advantage. I was tempted to sneak up behind her and push her off, but she was so strong I hadn't been able to budge her before. Besides, she'd probably just turn into a bird and . . . Hmm. A bird.

An idea formed in my mind. Yes, I do get ideas sometimes.

"Grover," I said, "can you use the lyre to summon a birdcage? Like a really strong one, made from Celestial bronze?"

He pursed his lips. "I suppose, but birds shouldn't be caged, Percy. They should be free! They should fly and—" He looked at the celedon. "Oh, you mean—"

"Yeah."

"I'll try."

"Good," I said. "Just wait for my cue. Do you still have that blindfold from Pin the Tail on the Human?"

He handed me the strip of cloth. I shrank my sword to ballpoint-pen form and slipped it in the pocket of my jeans. I'd need both hands free for this. I crept up on the celedon, who was now belting out the final chorus.

Even though she was facing the other way, her music filled me with the urge to dance (which, believe me, you never want to see). I forced myself to keep going, but fighting her magic was like pushing my way through a row of heavy drapes.

My plan was simple: Gag the celedon. She would turn

back into a bird and try to escape. I would grab her and shove her into a birdcage. What could go wrong?

On the last line of "New York, New York," I jumped on her back, locking my legs around her waist and yanking the blindfold across her mouth like a horse's bridle.

Her grand finale was cut short with a "New Yor—urff!"

"Grover, now!" I yelled.

The celedon stumbled forward. I had a dizzying view of the chaos below in Times Square—cops trying to clear the crowd, lines of tourists doing impromptu high-kick routines like the Radio City Rockettes. The electronic billboards down the side of the Times Tower looked like a very steep, psychedelic waterslide, with nothing but hard pavement at the bottom.

The celedon staggered backward, flailing and mumbling through the gag.

Grover desperately strummed his lyre. The strings sent powerful magic vibrations through the air, but Grover's voice quivered with uncertainty.

"Um, birds!" he warbled. "La, la, la! Birds in cages! Very strong cages! Birds!"

He wasn't going to win any Grammys with those lyrics, and I was losing my grip. The celedon was strong. I'd ridden a Minotaur before, and the golden lady was at least that hard to hold on to.

The celedon spun around, trying to throw me. She clamped her hands around my forearms and squeezed. Pain shot up to my shoulders.

I yelled, "Grover, hurry!" But with my teeth clenched, the words came out more like, "Grr—huh."

"Birds in cages!" Grover strummed another chord. "La, la, la, cages!"

Amazingly, a birdcage shimmered into being at the edge of the roof. I was too busy getting tossed around to have a good look, but Grover seemed to have done a good job. The cage was just large enough for a parrot, or a fat quail, and the bars glowed faintly . . . Celestial bronze.

Now if I could just get the celedon into bird form. Unfortunately, she wasn't cooperating. She spun hard, breaking my grip and shoving me over the side of the building.

I tried not to panic. Sadly, this wasn't the first time I'd been thrown off a skyscraper.

I'd like to tell you that I did some cool acrobatic move, grabbed the edge of a billboard, and vaulted back up to the roof in a perfect triple flip.

Nope. As I bounced off the first Jumbotron screen, a metal strut somehow snagged my belt and stopped me from falling. It also gave me the ultimate wedgie of all time. Then, as if that wasn't bad enough, my momentum spun me upside down and I peeled right out of my pants.

I plummeted headfirst toward Times Square, grabbing wildly for anything to slow me down. Luckily, the top of the next billboard had a rung across it, maybe for extremely brave maintenance workers to latch their harnesses onto.

I managed to catch it and flipped right side up. My arms were nearly yanked out of their sockets, but somehow I kept my grip. And that's how I ended up hanging from a billboard over Times Square without my pants.

To answer your next question: boxers. Plain blue boxers. No smiley faces. No hearts.

Laugh all you want. They're more comfortable than briefs.

The celedon smiled at me from the top of the roof, about twenty feet above. Just below her, my jeans hung from the metal strut, blowing in the wind like they were waving me goodbye. I couldn't see Grover. His music had stopped.

My grip weakened. The pavement was maybe seven hundred feet down, which would make for a very long scream as I fell to my death. The glowing screen of the Jumbotron was slowly cooking my stomach.

As I was dangling there, the celedon began a special

serenade just for me. She sang about letting go, laying down my troubles, resting by the banks of a river. I don't remember the exact lyrics, but you get the idea.

It was all I could do to hold on. I didn't want to drop, but the celedon's music washed over me, dismantling my resolve. I imagined that I would float down safely. I would land on the banks of a lazy river, where I could have a nice relaxing picnic with my girlfriend.

Annabeth.

I remembered the time I'd saved Annabeth from the Sirens in the Sea of Monsters. I'd held her while she cried and struggled, trying to swim to her death because she thought she would reach some beautiful promised land.

Now I imagined she was holding me back. I could hear what she'd say: *It's a trick, Seaweed Brain! You've got to trick her back or you'll die. And if you die, I'll never forgive you!*

That broke the celedon's spell. Annabeth's anger was way scarier than most monsters, but don't tell her I said that.

I looked up at my jeans, dangling uselessly above. My sword was in pen form in the pocket, where it did me no good. Grover had started to sing about birds again, but it wasn't helping. Apparently the celedon only turned into bird form when she was startled.

Wait . . .

Out of desperation, I formed Stupid Plan Version 2.0.

"Hey!" I called up. "You really are amazing, Miss Celedon! Before I die, can I have your autograph?"

The celedon halted midsong. She looked surprised, then smiled with pleasure.

"Grover!" I called. "Come over here!"

The lyre music stopped. Grover's head poked over the side. "Oh, Percy . . . I—I'm sorry—"

"It's okay!" I faked a smile, using our empathy link to tell him how I really felt. I couldn't send complete thoughts, but I tried to get the general point across: He needed to be ready. He needed to be quick. I hoped he was a good catch.

"Do you have a pen and paper?" I asked him. "I want to get this lady's autograph before I die."

Grover blinked. "Uh . . . jeez. No. But isn't there a pen in the pocket of your jeans?"

Best. Satyr. Ever. He totally got the plan.

"You're right!" I gazed up at the celedon imploringly. "Please? Last request? Could you just fish the pen out of my jeans and sign them? Then I can die happy."

Golden statues can't blush, but the celedon looked extremely flattered. She reached down, retrieved my jeans, and pulled out the pen.

I caught my breath. I'd never seen Riptide in the hands of a monster before. If this went wrong, if she realized it was a trick, she could kill Grover. Celestial bronze blades work just fine on satyrs.

She examined the pen like she'd never used one before.

"You have to take the cap off," I said helpfully. My fingers were beginning to slip.

She laid the jeans on the ledge, next to the birdcage. She uncapped the pen and Riptide sprang to life.

If I hadn't been about to die, it would've been the funniest thing I'd ever seen. You know those gag cans of candy with the coiled-up toy snake inside?

It was like watching somebody open one of those, except replace the toy snake with a three-foot-long blade.

The Celestial sword shot to full length and the celedon thrust it away, leaping backward with a not-very-musical shriek. She turned into a bird, but Grover was ready. He dropped Apollo's lyre and caught the fat golden quail in both hands.

Grover stuffed her in the cage and slammed the door shut. The celedon went crazy, squawking and flapping, but she didn't have room to turn back to human form, and in bird form—thank the gods—she didn't seem to have any magic in her voice.

"Good job!" I called up to Grover.

He looked sick. "I think I scratched Apollo's lyre. And I just caged a bird. This is the worst birthday ever."

"By the way," I reminded him, "I'm about to fall to my death here."

"Ah!" Grover snatched up the lyre and played a quick tune. Now that he wasn't in danger and the monster was caged, he seemed to have no problem using the lyre's magic. Typical. He summoned a rope and threw it down to me. Somehow he managed to pull me to the top, where I collapsed.

Below us, Times Square was still in complete chaos. Tourists wandered around in a daze. The cops were breaking up the last of the high-kick dance routines. A few cars were on fire, and the outdoor stage had been reduced to a pile of kindling, bricks, and broken sound equipment.

Across the Hudson River, the sun was going down. All I wanted to do was lie there on the roof and enjoy the feeling of not being dead. But our job wasn't done yet.

"We've got to get the celedon back to Apollo," I said.

"Yeah," Grover agreed. "But, uh . . . maybe put your pants on first?"

* * *

Apollo was waiting for us in the lobby of the Empire State Building. His three golden singers paced nervously behind him.

When he saw us, he brightened—literally. A glowing aura appeared around his head.

"Excellent!" He took the birdcage. "I'll get Hephaestus to fix her up, and this time I'm not taking any excuses about expired warranties. My show starts in half an hour!"

"You're welcome," I said.

Apollo accepted the lyre from Grover. The god's expression turned dangerously stormy. "You scratched it."

Grover whimpered. "Lord Apollo—"

"It was the only way to catch the celedon," I interceded. "Besides, it'll buff out. Get Hephaestus to do it. He owes you, right?"

For a second, I thought Apollo might blast us both to ashes, but finally he just grunted. "I suppose you're right. Well, good job, you two! As your reward, you're invited to watch me perform on Mount Olympus!"

Grover and I glanced at each other. Insulting a god was dangerous, but the last thing I wanted to do was hear more music.

"We aren't worthy," I lied. "We'd love to, really, but you know, we'd probably explode or something if we heard your godly music at full volume."

Apollo nodded thoughtfully. "You're right. It might distract from my performance if you exploded. How considerate of you." He grinned. "Well, I'm off, then. Happy birthday, Percy!"

"It's Grover's birthday," I corrected, but Apollo and his singers had already disappeared in a flash of golden light.

"So much for a day off," I said, turning back to Grover.

"Back to Prospect Park?" he suggested. "Juniper must be worried to death."

"Yeah," I agreed. "And I'm really hungry."

Grover nodded enthusiastically. "If we leave now, we can pick up Juniper and reach Camp Half-Blood in time for the sing-along. They have s'mores!"

I winced. "No sing-along, please. But I'll go for the s'mores."

"Deal!" Grover said.

I clapped him on the shoulder. "Come on, G-man. Your birthday might turn out okay after all."

BOUNCING THE GRINNING GOAT

BY SHANNON HALE

When I staggered into the town, I hadn't eaten in three days. My big brother's armor pressed heavy on my shoulders. His sword hung long from my belt, scraping the ground. I tripped over it, fell face-first into a mud puddle, and wondered, *If I just lay here, how long would it take me to die?*

The noon sun's heat on my back felt like a pat of encouragement. I found the energy to crawl back to my feet and stumble on, past houses, tanners, cobblers, and weavers, following the maddening smell of food. A tavern! Its carved wooden sign bore a smiling goat.

"Good morning, sir," I croaked at a short, round man

who was nailing a paper to the door.

I was about to ask—that is, *beg*—for a scrap of food when I read the notice he'd nailed up: BOUNCER WANTED.

A bouncer! If the job included meals, I could be a bouncer. Keep the tavern-goers in line, stop fights, toss out the troublemakers. After all, I looked after my nine little brothers and sisters. Or I had before I ran away.

"I'd like to be your bouncer," I said. "I know I don't look like much at the moment. . . ." I tried to scrape the mud off my face. "But I have excellent bouncer experience."

"Hmm, a stranger might work better than one of their own telling them what to do," he said. His voice was surprisingly high, like a morning bird's screech. "But what makes you think you could bounce my tavern any better than the last fellow?"

"What makes me think?" I made my face indignant. "What makes me think?"

The wind shifted, blowing rich scents from the tavern kitchen—charred beef, bacon grease, milky potato stew, oat muffins. My stomach shrank one more size. Just then, I'd have said *anything* to get fed, but the first solution that popped into my mind was—

"I'm from Old Hollow."

The little man blinked twice and took a step back. "Old

H-h-hollow? Oh my oh my." He rubbed his hands together and looked everywhere but my face. "Yes, yes, an Old Hollower. That'll do. Oh my, yes."

He didn't ask for proof. After all, who would *dare* falsely claim to be an Old Hollower? The twisting of my thin stomach took up so much of my attention I didn't feel guilty yet. Because I was actually from *New* Hollow, which is just down the mountain and on the other side of the wood. But we shared the same stream, so that sort of counted, didn't it?

No, it didn't. I'd never seen an Old Hollower, but I'd heard the tales—they fought with swords forged of hot light, their eyes burned like fire to see through lies, they could turn into living flame and chase away their enemies. New Hollowers like me were normal boring folk.

"Welcome to Bendy Stream," said the little man. "I'm Churn. What was your name?"

My big brothers all got warrior names like Forge, Strike, and Tackle, while I got—

"Spark," I said. It sounded like something you would swat away—a firefly or flitting ash. I suppose it could have been worse. My little sisters were named Ponder, Silence, Listen, and Behave. By the way, Behave was the naughtiest four-year-old in the Five Kingdoms.

I tried to sound casual as I asked, "Now, about meals . . ."

"You can eat after work," said Churn.

My belly made a pathetic squeak.

Inside, the tavern was smoky from the hearth fire and as dark as evening. At this time of day, our little tavern back home would be mostly empty, but the Grinning Goat was half-full of people eating their noon meal.

The salty scent of meat made me wobble. I grabbed a chair back. It'd be hard to look fearsome while in a dead faint.

"Hey!" Churn screeched. "Hey!"

The talking and clanking died down.

Churn adjusted his apron. "You all know what happened to my last bouncer, rest him, though maybe only one of you knows exactly how he ended up in that ditch."

The last bouncer was . . . dead? My legs tried to fold beneath me.

"But never you mind because my new bouncer isn't going to put up with your fighting and thieving and accumulating of excessive meal tabs. *This* one is an Old Hollower."

The silence got silenter.

Please feed me, I wanted to beg, but I guessed that tactic would get me tossed out the door. I needed to convince them I was an Old Hollower. I did have some practice in storytelling. The little ones wouldn't go to sleep without a good story.

"Greetings, Bendy Stream!" I said grandly. "I am Mistress Spark." My stomach let out a groan so loud it could've been a dragon's snore. I tried to cover it with a cough. "As you can see, I'm young, and the powers of young Hollowers are still raw. If I were forced to fight you, I might hurt you terribly. So let's just avoid fighting at all costs. Um, thank you."

Someone whispered, "That little girl is a Hollower?"

"Looks more like a half-drowned rat than a mage," someone else whispered.

"So . . . so let's just all be nice," I said not as grandly. "If you don't mind. Please."

I put my shaking hands in my pockets and gripped my lucky rock.

"Hey, Blaze," I heard a man whisper, "I dare you to shove her over and see what happens."

Years ago I'd found my lucky rock on the mountain— black, big as a duck egg, its irregular facets smooth like glass. On boring winter days back home, I used the rock to reflect a spot of sun or firelight onto the ground, wiggling it for the little ones to chase. Old Hollower powers seemed to involve light. Could I fool this lot with a light trick?

I stepped into the brightest spot in the room, where sunlight poured through the window. I held the rock down low by my side.

"You!" I said, pointing to the man who had just spoken. When he looked at me, I twisted the rock, reflecting light into his eyes.

"Aah," he said, squinting.

"And you, and you, and you," I said, reflecting that bright light directly into the eyes of three more people. "I've marked you four with my . . . my light mage powers. *Ahem.* That was just a flutter of magic. You don't want to feel my, uh, full wrath."

I slipped the rock back into my pocket. The four I'd shined were shielding their eyes, afraid to look at me.

"I'm not going to blind you. Today." I smiled. "Just be nice and you have nothing to worry about. All settled? All right, let's eat up!"

Everyone went back to their meals, whispering about the Old Hollower bouncer.

At the bar, Churn took out a wooden bowl. I took a step closer. He ladled not one, but two whole scoops of stew into the bowl, topping it with half a torn loaf of dark, nutty bread. I felt drool trickle out the corner of my mouth.

"Eat up, Mistress Spark," he said. "The evening crowd is worse."

I fell onto the bar stool and shoveled in the first spoonful. The stew was very hot and full of venison, cabbage, and carrots cooked so long they fell apart on my tongue. A tear dropped from my eye into the bowl, adding a little more salt. I hoped no one noticed the fierce Hollower bouncer crying.

Once the noon meal passed, most of the folk went back to work in their shops and fields. I stayed on the bar stool. Now that I hadn't died of hunger, I wanted to die of shame. Old Hollower? Really, Spark?

When the sun began setting, Churn's girls lit the oil lamps, the fat burning smoky and bitter. And the tavern filled. Every table, every chair, the upper floor as rowdy as the lower.

Hollower, people whispered, talking behind their hands.

I felt like a bug in a bird's nest.

A broad-shouldered woman stalked up to me, fists on her hips. "Prove that you're an Old Hollower," she said.

Prove it how? It was too dark to do a light trick with my rock. At home when the little ones seemed especially sneaky, I would shout, "I know what you're doing," even when I didn't. But they'd get spooked and stop whatever mischief they'd had planned.

So I leaned close and whispered to this woman, "I know what you've done." And I pointed at her.

The woman blushed. She looked down and hurried away. I exhaled.

The crowd ate. They sang to a musician's flute. They danced and drank and shouted and shoved. Someone threw a punch.

"Stop that!" I said, standing on my stool. The punchers backed down. For now. But how long could I keep this up?

"Spark, come talk to Mister Grunt," Churn called to me. "Mister Grunt owes coin for a month's worth of meals."

Grunt was twice as tall as me and four times as big, bulging with studded leather armor and a ridiculously huge war hammer. He was hunched over his meal at the bar, stabbing chunks of stew with a pointed bone knife, drinking broth from the bowl and dribbling it into his beard. His beard was so filthy I thought washing it with stew could only be an improvement.

"Mister Grunt," I said in my stern tone. "Pay Mister Churn."

Grunt wiped his mouth with his sleeve, looked at me hard and said, "No."

I pressed my hands to my stomach and felt as skinny

as my own skeleton under my armor. I tried the pointing thing again.

"What?" said Grunt, scowling at my pointing finger.

"Pay up," I said, still pointing.

"Or what?" he said.

I had no idea or what, but my, did he have lovely hair. Long, black, shockingly curly—

"Or—or your hair will fall out," I spluttered.

I noticed the tavern had gotten real quiet. Grunt leaned close to my face, his breath sticky with ale.

"I fought in the Southern Wars, Spark," he said, spittle flying with my name. "I've seen *real* Hollowers."

My heart was beating like a jackrabbit's. I tried to smile as if I had all the confidence in the world, probably just managing to look like I urgently needed the outhouse.

"Well?" Churn asked me. "How come his hair isn't falling out?"

"M-magic doesn't always work fast." I said.

I pretended I did need to use the outhouse, but then I ran into the dark woods behind it.

Running away again, Spark? Where would I go this time? Just two days from home my food had run out. I hadn't managed to catch any game, and no nuts, berries, or roots conveniently appeared to feed me. I'd spent the past three nights starving, shivering, afraid the creaking of the woods was the sound of Ash Raiders out on the hunt.

I couldn't go home, even if my brother Forge wouldn't kill me for stealing his armor, even if I could be happy in our crowded house again—Mama shouting at me to help her corral the little ones, make sure they didn't drown in the stream, wipe their noses and bottoms. I'd never survive the return trip without food.

I looked at my boot (Forge's boot, actually, with an extra sock stuffed in the toe). I'd stepped on a darkease plant. At home when one of us was sick, Mama would give us darkease tea to help us rest peaceful through the night.

I went back into the Grinning Goat and served Grunt some stew myself. I may have crushed certain leaves into his bowl.

"This is your last meal at the Grinning Goat until you pay Churn every coin you owe," I said.

Grunt laughed.

He stumbled home at closing time. I followed, sneaking from shadow to shadow. When I squeaked his door open, Grunt snored and rolled over on his bed.

I was well practiced for this trick. I used to help shear Papa's sheep. But it really was a shame to cut off all that beautiful curly hair.

The next evening when Grunt entered the Grinning Goat, the music cut short. The laughing, shouting, and hollering silenced. Everyone stared at Grunt's bare scalp, as white as a winter rabbit.

Grunt emptied his coin bag on the bar. Churn filled up a horn with frothy ale. Grunt turned to the room, lifted the horn, and shouted, "To Mistress Spark, our very own Hollower!"

The room erupted in cheers.

I blushed. Some of that blush was shame. I'd promised Churn I'd help keep the Grinning Goat in line. It didn't matter that I was lying to get it done, did it?

Grunt pulled me aside, bending in half to reach my ear. "Will it grow back?"

"Yes," I said.

He rubbed his bare head and sniffed. "Good. I kind of liked my hair."

For two more weeks I bounced the Grinning Goat. By day the patrons gave me little trouble. I would sit in the sun by the window, slowly drinking a horn of milk. I held my lucky rock, and its glassy darkness seemed not to reflect but actually to soak up the light. I made up stories about its origin—was it really a dragon's eye? A shard from a

Hollower flame sword? An Ash Raider's black stony heart?

I didn't use my rock to flash light at troublemakers anymore. After Grunt, the only trick I needed was to point and holler some. I ate three meals a day. I got used to not hearing Mama's voice yelling, "Spark, go check on your brothers! Wash the dishes! My hands are full, I need you to see which baby is stinky!" In fact I barely thought about home at all.

Until one afternoon when in stalked the most frightening sight I'd ever laid eyes on.

It was my big brother Forge, whose armor I was currently wearing and whose sword I'd scratched so badly trying to practice fight a rock that I'd stuffed it under my mattress out of embarrassment.

His gaze was raking the tavern, searching for me. I turned away. I started toward the back—

"Spark!"

I froze.

I could hear Forge's boots stomping across the tavern's floor. Or maybe they were our brother Bluster's boots, since I was wearing Forge's.

Grunt stepped between me and Forge. "You want to mess with our bouncer?" he said. "Then you mess with Grunt. I'm *her* bouncer."

My "big" brother Forge had never looked so tiny.

I'd been closer to Forge than any of my brothers and sisters. We were the only ones born without a twin. "We lonely babes need to stick together," he used to say. Until I stole his armor and ran away into the night.

"I . . . I . . ." Forge was saying. Grunt had unhooked his war hammer.

"It's all right, Grunt," I said. "This is my brother. Excuse us a moment."

I pulled Forge by his sleeve into the leaf-speckled sunlight beyond the tavern. He looked so achingly familiar—the dark brown eyes we all shared, the whiskers just growing on his lip and chin, the brow scar I'd given him years ago when playing with a wood sword. I wondered if I looked any different to him.

"If you're going to kill me, do it here, please," I said. "Otherwise Grunt will fight you, and that'll get messy."

Forge rolled his eyes. "Spark, what happened? Everyone assumed you'd gotten up in the night to use the outhouse and had been carried off by a pack of wolves."

"They did?" Being savaged by a wild beast was a nice, dramatic way to die. Though of course I'd prefer a valiant death in a hopeless but noble battle.

"Then I noticed my armor was missing. My precious

armor I'd sweated and worked for and rubbed with oil every single night. . . ."

I whimpered. "I'm sorry, Forge."

"Why'd you leave, Spark?" Forge sounded more sad than angry.

"Why wouldn't I? The world is full of adventures, but I was stuck in that crazy, crowded house watching over nine little ones who were constantly fighting—"

"So you're better off in this crazy, crowded tavern watching over dozens of big ones who are constantly fighting?"

"Um . . ." He had an excellent point.

I'd always been plagued with warrior dreams. In one I stood atop a mountain facing down an entire army—and I wasn't hopeless. In the dream, I won! So I'd left home hoping I'd stumble into a marvelous adventure. The Grinning Goat had great stew, but wasn't I the same girl here I'd always been?

"Come home with me," Forge said.

I shook my head. My big brothers complained about their warrior training and farming chores. They had no idea what it was like being the oldest girl in a big family.

But then he said, "Mama misses you, Spark. She cries at night."

Mama cried? Over me? I was the middle of sixteen. I

didn't think she'd even notice I was gone.

My eyes stung. I didn't want to cry, so I looked up at the sun to dry away the sting.

"Stop that," said Forge. "I hate when you do that. It's creepy."

Staring at the sun was supposed to turn anyone blind, but it never hurt my eyes. I loved how warm and strong the sun made me feel, like that fierce light could fill me up.

"I'll come home," I said real quiet so my voice wouldn't crack. I couldn't quite believe I was giving up on my adventure already, but if Mama missed me, I'd always go home.

"Spark!" Grunt came barreling through the brush, loud as a bull. "Spark, the Ash Raiders are coming this way."

Forge stood up from a tree stump so fast, he tripped and stepped on my boots. *His* boots, actually.

"Did you say the Ash Raiders are coming this way?" I asked.

I was hoping Grunt actually had said something like "the trash traders are coming to pay" and I'd simply misheard.

"Yeah," he said, and my heart plunged into Forge's boots. Grunt kept looking over his shoulder, as if afraid the raiders had already arrived. "Some people just ran into town from Two Toads, the village to the north. The Ash Raiders burned Two Toads to the ground. The survivors said the raiders were moving south."

"That's . . . that's terrible," I said. "I guess this is perfect timing for me to go home then."

"But you can't go now." Grunt's frown made his beard bushier. "If we don't fight, they'll steal and burn everything. And you're our best chance to beat them. I mean, you are an Old Hollower."

A *New* Hollower, I thought. And New Hollow had as much magic as cold oatmeal.

Forge was frowning. "Wait, what's all this about Old Holl—"

I backhanded Forge in the stomach. "Not now, we've got a crisis," I said. "Grunt, how many armed fighters in Bendy Stream?"

"Two dozen."

Would that be enough? I'd wanted an adventure. I'd wanted a dramatic and glorious battle. But I didn't figure I'd find one so soon, or one quite so dramatic and glorious.

"You won't stand alone against the raiders," said Forge. "Count my sword among your own. That is, as soon as Spark gives it back to me."

"That's nice, but . . ." Grunt blushed. "Everyone voted at the Grinning Goat. They're mighty afraid of the Ash Raiders, and they'd all just rather you fought them yourself,

Mistress Spark. You and your Hollower brother."

I stared at Grunt so hard he took a step back, covering his head with his hands as if afraid I'd fry off the black fuzz that was just growing back. The lot of them were planning to throw me and Forge at the raiders? We'd be slaughtered!

I marched back into the tavern, stood on the landing, and with my hands on my hips, I shouted, "Quiet down! Do you hear me talking to you? I said QUIET DOWN!"

I sounded so much like my mama I gave myself chills. All I needed was a wooden spoon to smack a few bottoms.

"You expect me and my brother to stop the Ash Raiders alone?" I said. "You bunch of lazy, spoiled, good-for-nothing louses. I'm ashamed of the lot of you. Ashamed!"

A few heads hung down. I nodded, satisfied.

"I know you'd like us to magically make them go away, but we can't. We'll stand beside you, but you'll need to fight like mad. So let's get to work or by my left toe, some heads will roll."

And I followed up with some serious pointing.

There was no way everyone was more afraid of little me than of the Ash Raiders. At my most fearsome I'd shined a light in a few eyes. The Ash Raiders had burned dozens of towns to the ground, stolen livestock, and run the people off to starve in the wilderness. But the townsfolk listened to me anyway. What nice folk they were. I really didn't want to see their town burned.

I was going to need more than a lucky rock and a couple darkease leaves. Defeating the Ash Raiders called for some serious tricks. With Churn and Forge's help, I assigned everyone a task: gathering weapons and tools, digging ditches, wrapping arrows with ale-dipped cloth, building a barricade on the north side of the town's main road.

We gathered the outlying farm families in and for two days all Bendy Streamers stayed in the center of town, taking turns at cooking, cleaning, digging, prepping, and watching.

It was morning when a girl appropriately named Scout came running from her scouting post.

"They're here!" she said, out of breath. "They're—"

That was all the warning we got. Over the horizon flowed the Ash Raiders.

They rode horses and bulls. Their clothes were black. Their hair and faces were smeared with the ashes of towns they'd razed. Sunlight glinted off swords and hammers, axes and arrow points. I tried to count them all but I got dizzy.

The townsfolk huddled behind our barricade of stacked wagons. I'm certain I wasn't the only one shivering under the bright sun.

"Is this an adventure?" I whispered to Forge.

"Yes," he said.

"Is it supposed to be fun?" I asked.

"Not at the moment," he said.

"Good," I said. "I was afraid I was doing it wrong."

I stepped out in front.

"I'm an Old Hollower!" I shouted. "Retreat while you can!"

They kept coming. Well, it had been worth a try.

A raider on horseback disappeared into the middle of the street. I pointed at him as if I'd made him disappear with my spectacular mage powers. Actually I'd asked Grunt and others to dig random ditches all down the street, fill them with water, and sprinkle dirt on top for camouflage. Another rider plunged into a water hole. And another. I pointed. I pointed.

The raiders didn't seem fooled. They kept coming.

Our longbowmen lit their arrows on fire and shot them in high arcs.

"Ha-ha!" I shouted. "Fear the light magic of Old Hollow!"

Some of our arrows hit the raiders, black clothing catching fire. But the rest of the raiders kept coming.

I had only one trick left. I motioned to Forge and several others and we lifted metal shields. I'd assigned the children of the town to polish them till they were extra shiny. We tilted the shields, reflecting sunlight into the eyes of the Ash Raiders' front line.

"I blind you!" I shouted. "I blind you with my mage powers!"

Several broke off and fled. But the rest were not afraid. They shielded their eyes and kept coming.

"Mistress Spark?" Grunt looked hopefully at me, his eyes small in his huge face. "Let me have a go."

I didn't want to say yes. I wanted to be a real Hollower and win the day! But I nodded.

Grunt lifted his hammer and shouted. His two dozen warriors ran forward, meeting the first line. Grunt took out two raiders in one swipe. But there were so many.

I felt a tug on my shirt. (Forge's shirt, actually.) Scout was beside me, her big eyes pleading.

"That's my papa," she said, pointing to a thin, grizzly-bearded man with a rake, standing with the nonfighters. "He says he'll have to fight since your powers weren't enough. But you won't make him, right? You'll stop the raiders yourself because you're a Hollower, right?"

Why can't some lies be true?

I gazed at the black wall of killers marching at us and my gaze got lost in their vastness. Grunt's warriors would never be enough.

"We have to retreat!" I shouted back at the village. The

warriors would give us time to get the rest of the townsfolk away. We had no choice but to abandon Bendy Stream.

We started to run away from the raiders, but suddenly we were running toward them. Because more raiders were entering town from the other side. We were surrounded by a sea of black, pushing us in. They wouldn't only steal all the goods and burn the town, they'd burn the townsfolk inside it.

I couldn't let that happen. I couldn't. I had to do something, something, something. . . .

I gripped my lucky rock in my pocket. I felt the sun above, so hot, the heat a slap on the top of my head.

Forge ran back to me from the fighting. "I promised Mama I'd bring you home. Come on. We can't win here, Spark. They're as big as the night."

Nothing can stop night but the sun.

I climbed atop the barricade of wagons. I climbed and I climbed and I lifted my lucky rock up. Could I make a lie real?

"Spark!" I could hear Forge calling. It was nice that he was afraid for me, but I didn't look down. The sun had always felt like kin, and I followed the hot, crazy nagging that the sun could help. I imagined not just reflecting the light but pulling it into my rock. My fingers and palms burned, but it felt good, like clutching a mug of warm milk after playing in the snow.

"Spark! Get down!"

The black rock brightened.

A group of raider bowmen galloped toward the barricade, a glint of arrows, bowstrings pulled back, aiming at me.

"Leave!" I shouted.

They didn't leave. The raiders loosed their arrows.

I loosed the sun.

Light exploded from the rock and shot from my fingers. My white, too-bright burst met the arrows midway, swallowing them up. The burst kept sizzling down the road and rolled over the raider bowmen. I heard screeches of fear, their mounts screaming and stamping. Smoke rose from the raiders' black clothes, the ash fizzled from their hair. The first group fled.

"Grunt, get back!" I shouted.

He and his men retreated, and I pulled sunlight into the rock and shot it at the raider swordsmen. The burst crackled over their heads and chased them away.

I aimed now for the raiders who were hedging in the townsfolk.

"Leave!" I said. By the time my white burst reached the remaining Ash Raiders, they were already fleeing. In moments the last one had disappeared under the horizon.

My eyes were dazzled. I blinked several times and looked down. The whole town was staring at me.

"Yep," said Grunt, "that's what I saw Hollowers do in the Southern Wars."

Forge had climbed up beside me. His mouth was as wide open as his eyes.

"Before I left, Mama said she named you Spark because you had the spark. At the time, I didn't know what she meant."

This was all feeling right, the waking world moving just like it did in my dreams.

Forge and I didn't linger another day in Bendy Stream. I hugged and kissed all the Grinning Goat regulars. Churn sniffled as he gave me a week's worth of travel food. Grunt followed us to the edge of town and waved till I could no longer make out his fuzzy black head.

Forge and I were going home. I couldn't stand to make Mama sad. But on the way, we would pass through Old Hollow. Just to say hello. And maybe ask them about my lucky rock and how I was able to hold the sun.

THE SCOUT
BY D. J. MACHALE

Kit was on his own.

That was his first mistake.

He was the kind of guy who didn't follow the rules, especially if he saw no good reason to. He wasn't a trouble-maker, but unlike most of his friends, who blindly bowed to authority, he made his decisions based on what common sense told him was right . . . even when he was the only one who felt that way.

His latest misadventure began innocently enough on a camping trip with his Scout troop. The plan was to leave their base with a group of thirteen Scouts and two Leaders on a two-day excursion through rocky, desertlike terrain to practice survival skills. Kit didn't see the point other than to earn a badge that he couldn't have cared less about. He laughed at the Scouts who proudly displayed their awards on a sash that proved they could swim a mile or treat wounds or repeatedly hit a bull's-eye. Kit could do all those things, better than most. He just didn't feel the need to show off his accomplishments by sporting colorful badges. He knew what he was capable of and that was good enough for him.

The Scout Leaders didn't agree. They wanted their young charges to compete with one another, which was why Kit found himself trudging across the blazing desert with a light backpack along with twelve other sweaty Scouts. He wanted to be somewhere else, anywhere else, but with two Leaders keeping a watchful eye on every move they made there was no way he could dodge what was sure to be a grueling, pointless couple of days.

It was hot. Torturous, nasty, pass-out hot. That didn't stop the Leaders from driving the boys deep into the desert. Five miles, ten miles. They passed towering cliffs and crossed bone-dry riverbeds. Rationing water was crucial. Each Scout started off with a small bottle of water that had to last until they found resources in the desert, which wasn't easy. The Leaders instructed them to keep their mouths moist by sucking on small pebbles to activate their salivary glands. Kit was way ahead of them. He had been working on a couple of pebbles long before the Leaders offered the tip. He wanted to point out that if this were a true survival situation they wouldn't be hiking, like idiots, during the heat of the day. Instead they would be resting in the shade to conserve energy and reduce their sweat output. But this wasn't his show, so he quietly went along.

He made a point of veering into the shade whenever possible, even if it meant adding a few extra steps. He didn't talk, unlike the others, who were laughing and joking from the get-go. Kit wondered if the Leaders realized how much precious energy they were wasting. It seemed to him that they were driving the Scouts hard and letting them make dumb mistakes. But why? Was it another test? Another competition? Or did they just want to push them to the brink of dehydration and exhaustion for fun? It sure seemed that way. Or maybe the Leaders were just as clueless as the Scouts. Whatever the case, Kit wasn't about to do anything that would make the adventure any worse than it already was, so he kept his mouth shut and sucked on his pebbles.

Once they had hiked farther into the desert than Kit had ever been before, the true rules of the excursion were revealed. It was indeed a competition. The Leaders split the group in two. Each would take half the Scouts and march in a different direction. Whichever group fared better would be treated to an exceptional meal when they returned to base. The losers would be left to watch with envy.

Kit had no idea who would be the judge or what the criteria for winning might be and didn't care. What he saw was an opportunity. The Scouts were split up . . . seven in one group and six in the other. Kit made sure he was with the group of seven. Soon after the two teams went in different directions he marched up to his Leader and requested permission to join the *other* group. He explained that his good friend was with them and he worried that his buddy might be in over his head. He asked permission to join them so he could look out for the guy. The Leader complimented Kit on his leadership qualities and sent him on his way to catch up with the others.

Kit didn't have a close friend in the other group.

He had no intention of joining them.

What he wanted was to be on his own, and with both Leaders thinking he was with the other, he got his wish.

Once certain that he couldn't be seen by either group, he pulled off his pack, found some shade, and got off his feet. He wasn't thrilled about having to spend two days in the desert alone, but knew he was far better off on his own than trudging along with a bunch of clueless rookies. His plan was to lay low, conserve his energy and his water, then march back into camp and announce that he had gotten lost but managed to survive with no help. Who knows? Maybe he'd even be declared the winner of the dumb contest.

Kit put up his feet and relaxed, comfortable for the first time in hours and confident that his adventure in the desert was going to be far less torturous than if he had followed the rules.

Digging through his pack he saw that the Scouts had equipped him with a few essential survival tools: a long length of light rope, a thin reflective blanket, a simple first aid kit, flint and steel to spark a fire, a small hunting knife, and an item that was only to be used in a dire emergency . . . a communication device. If he were truly in trouble he could use it to call for help. The Leaders may have wanted to push the Scouts to the limit and test their abilities, but they also wanted everyone back alive.

Kit had no intention of using the device. He was going to make it on his own, whether or not he would be rewarded with an official badge or a special meal.

Knowing that as soon as night fell the desert temperature would plunge from searing hot to bone-numbing cold,

Kit erected a simple shelter using lengths of scrub that he propped against a wall of rust-colored rock. He gathered kindling and found enough dry wood to use as fuel. With a few quick flicks of metal on stone, he sparked up the tinder and in minutes he had a crackling fire that would keep him warm during the long desert night.

Sunset came quickly. It was stunning, complete with long streaks of orange and lavender clouds that hung above the distant mountains. When the sun dropped from sight the temperature dropped with it, but Kit felt warm and secure with his fire and shelter. He planned to get up early and search for food and water in the cool morning hours, though he wasn't stressed about it. He knew that if he came up empty he'd still be okay. He'd been hungry before. Gutting it out for two days wouldn't be a problem.

Kit stretched out in the shelter with his head resting on his pack and only his thoughts to keep him company. With his mind completely clear, his thoughts turned once again to a difficult decision he had been weighing for months: He wanted to quit the Scouts. His parents had forced him to join, saying it was every guy's duty to serve. Kit had signed up to make his folks happy but never bought into the Scout culture. He loved being outdoors and had made several good friends, but he didn't see any purpose to the regimentation and military-like training. It wasn't his style. Quitting would upset his parents for sure, and the Leaders would do their best to convince him to stay, but he wasn't sure if he could stick it out until his mission was complete.

His mission.

It was the only reason he had stuck it out with the Scouts as long as he had.

Kit lay back and looked up to the night sky. Being in the desert, away from the glow of civilization, he saw more stars than he ever remembered seeing before. An endless canopy of lights spread from horizon to horizon. It was so incredibly clear that Kit felt as if he could gaze through them to the other side of the universe. The immensity of it all was both staggering and humbling as he tried to comprehend how many different worlds he might be viewing. How many civilizations? How many people? How many lives were beginning and ending at that exact moment? He wondered which of the twinkling spots held life and which were nothing more than gaseous, burning masses . . . and how many people were out there staring back at him, wondering the exact same thing? The idea that he might be gazing at multiple living worlds was a staggering concept that was hard to imagine, since he couldn't see any actual signs of life.

Or could he?

A single, shimmering "star" moved across the sky. At first he thought his eyes were playing tricks and it was the residual impression left by another bright star. He blinked, but it was still there, moving steadily and quickly. Kit sat up and tracked it until it disappeared behind the distant ridge of mountains. The sight threw him. Speculating about the potential for life while gazing at a billion stars was one thing; seeing an actual sign of intelligent life speeding by was far more dramatic. What could it have been? A satellite? A space station orbiting the globe? Or was it a craft from another planet swinging by to take a peek at his home?

Seeing that tiny speck of light moving through the sky fired Kit's imagination. There was life out there. He knew that. Everybody knew that. Reaching out to it was something he had dreamed of since he was old enough to put his eye to a telescope. That ambition still burned, and it took a simple moving light to remind him of that . . . and to question his thoughts about quitting the Scouts. As much as he didn't appreciate their methods and rigid regulations, they offered him the best chance to touch the stars.

His thoughts were suddenly alive with possibilities, which made falling asleep next to impossible. But that was okay. Kit liked thinking through challenges, and there was no better time to do it than while he was alone, staring at a sky full of stars. He lay back, let his mind float up to the heavens, and eventually drifted off to sleep.

He might have slept through the night and well into the next day if it hadn't been for a loud explosion that shattered the tranquility of the desert. Kit sat up immediately, crashing his head into the branches of his shelter. What was that? He hadn't dreamed it, for he could still hear its echo drifting over the barren landscape. It was morning. The sun had barely crept over the mountains, so the temperature had yet to begin its inevitable climb. He shivered. His campfire had long since burned out, and his thin Scout uniform did little to provide warmth.

The slight discomfort was the last thing on his mind. He scrambled to his feet and quickly climbed onto the rock where he had built his lean-to. He stood on top and scanned the desert, doing a slow 360, looking for anything that might have created the boom. There was nothing to see but miles of scrub and sand and rock. He waited and listened in case another explosion followed. He heard nothing but the wind and the far-off cries of birds in search of their morning meal.

He shrugged and was about to jump down when his eye

caught movement. Not on the ground; in the sky. A dark speck appeared that at first looked like a hovering bird. But birds didn't hover. He watched with curiosity and soon realized that it was growing closer. Fast. Whatever it was, it was falling. It didn't appear to have aerodynamic capability. Or power. Whatever it was, it was freefalling . . . and headed for Kit.

There was less chance of getting hit by a falling meteor than getting struck by lightning, but Kit wasn't taking chances. He jumped down from the rock and pressed against it for protection.

The mysterious mass grew larger. Kit realized that if it were indeed a meteor, the explosion could have been the sonic boom it created when it tore through the atmosphere, faster than the speed of sound.

As it dropped ever closer to the ground, Kit could make out detail . . . enough to prove that it was not a meteor after all. Its shape was too perfect. It looked to be made up of several uniformly round spheres that were connected together to form a mass that resembled a bunch of grapes. That meant it was manmade. The realization brought him back to the point of light he had seen moving through the night sky. Was this the object he had seen? The plummeting device could be a satellite whose orbit had decayed enough for gravity to grab hold and pull it back home.

The object was going to miss him by a few hundred yards. Confident that he wasn't in danger, Kit climbed back up onto the rock to get the best view of the descent. He wondered if the other Scouts were watching . . . wherever they were. They had to have heard the sonic boom.

The falling mass was seconds from crashing. Kit braced for a violent impact followed by total destruction. He wondered if the spheres would break apart and scatter across the desert floor, and he tensed up, ready to dive out of the way in case any exploded debris came his way.

There was a brief whistling sound . . . and then it hit.

The object didn't break up. It bounced. The entire mass was launched back into the air, intact. The collection of spheres spun wildly, the force of impact sending it twisting and turning. It looked more like a child's toy than a mysterious object that had fallen from space. It sailed impossibly high before gravity took hold once more and pulled it back to hit the ground and bounce again.

Kit jumped down from his observation platform and took off running toward it.

The object continued to bounce, each time hitting with less energy and getting less height. It soon stopped launching altogether and tumbled wildly over the uneven desert floor. When it was finally close to settling, the object bounced off a sheer wall of rock and rolled into a wide, dry riverbed . . . falling down and out of sight.

Kit sprinted across the scrubby sand, leaping over small rocks and dodging gnarled trees. He no longer cared about using energy or wasting precious fluid. His curiosity had blasted those worries out of his head. After running flat out for nearly five minutes, he slowed when he neared the edge of the culvert where the object had disappeared. The thought struck him that if it were a failed spacecraft there might be toxic fumes or spilled fuel or any number of other dangerous substances that he would be wise to avoid. He had learned all about such things as part of his training. He slowed to a walk, then crept forward and peered cautiously over the edge.

The craft, or whatever it was, lay jammed against the far edge of the deep, dry riverbed. There was no hiss of escaping gas or metallic ticking from a cooling engine. The large device appeared to be as low-tech as could be, still looking like a massive bunch of grapes. Each of the dark-gray spheres was two feet in diameter, making the overall size of the wreck close to that of a small truck. There were no markings or identifying numbers printed anywhere. Two of the spheres had been damaged during the crash and hung like deflated balloons. That spoke volumes. This device was designed to do exactly what it had done . . . bounce. The shredded spheres showed that they were fabricated out of something soft but durable. They dangled like limp rags in front of an opening that had been torn apart during the tumultuous crash.

Kit slid down the near-vertical side of the culvert until he was on the same level as the wreck. It appeared much larger and more daunting than when he had been looking down on it from above. Kit made his way slowly, cautiously, toward the mass and the gash in its side that would reveal its contents. He didn't expect there to be a living person inside. Nobody could have survived such a violent landing.

Kit continued to move closer, staring at the gaping black opening. He stopped a few feet away, knelt down on one knee, then leaned over and peered inside.

Black. That's all he could see. He leaned forward and reached his hand out to touch one of the spheres. It was indeed soft, but rugged.

A single green light flashed on inside. Kit jumped back in surprise, landing on his butt. He quickly crawled away backward, afraid of . . . what? An alien creature with a scrambled brain that might reach out and grab him? A moment later he heard the slight whine of a machine powering to life. Something was inside. Kit was torn between fear and curiosity. Both prevented him from moving.

The whirring sound grew louder. Whatever was in there, it was firing up.

There was a loud metallic clicking sound followed by the complete self-disassembly of the craft. It was as if a latch had been released that had been holding the spheres together. The balls that were clustered together simultaneously fell away and tumbled across the dry riverbed, rolling and bouncing every which way. One rolled up to Kit, and he instinctively kicked it away. They seemed harmless, but he couldn't be sure. They bounced off each other and rolled like oversize toys, scattering across the culvert until they eventually came to rest.

What remained of the wreck was a rigid wire frame.

Inside the skeleton, on the ground, was a large toy.

It was a miniature truck, but like nothing Kit had ever seen before. It stood about two feet high with six wire wheels that looked as though they could handle most any terrain. Above the wheels was a flat, black, rectangular slab that was roughly eight inches thick. The top surface was shiny smooth. Surrounding the body were silver tubes, stacked three high, running the length of each side. The green light glowed from beneath the body, above the array of wheels.

It was a miniature all-terrain vehicle.

Kit sat in the dusty culvert, staring at the small truck. Where had it come from? Was it a military experiment gone awry? Was it part of the survival training? Or was there something more incredible going on? Had this come from deep space? If so, why did it crash here? Was it intentional or a mistake?

The device didn't move. Neither did Kit. He had plenty of questions and not a single answer . . . but he knew how to start asking. He reached into the cargo pocket on his thigh and pulled out his communicator. The Scouts had been told to use the device only in an emergency. Kit wasn't sure if this qualified and didn't care. He pressed and held the power button, waiting for the device to boot up. His plan was to report the crash to the Scout Leaders back at base and request that they send out a team to investigate. They could use the signal from his communicator to pinpoint his position.

As far as he was concerned, the survival exercise was over.

Kit glanced at his communicator, expecting to see the display of icons that led to its various functions. What he saw instead was static. He shook the device. It didn't help. There was power, but no function. He was about to turn it off and on again . . .

. . . when the whirring sound of the little machine's engines grew louder. The wheels remained stationary as the body above them slowly rotated forty-five degrees, then stopped. The silver tubes that ran along the two longer sides pivoted away from the body until the three ends on one side were facing forward and the opposite three were facing back.

The three facing forward . . . were facing Kit.

Kit stared into the dark mouths of the tubes.

There was a short, sharp whine as if the machine were powering up.

Those few seconds saved Kit's life.

He reacted more out of instinct than training. He dove to his right as a focused blast of energy erupted from the device's front-facing tubes, sending out an invisible salvo that hit the wall of the culvert behind the spot where Kit had been sitting, creating an eruption of dirt and rock that blew high into the sky.

Kit lay on his belly, shocked and paralyzed with fear as dirt and debris rained down on him. The machine slowly rotated, once again aiming its silver tubes at him . . . tubes that had revealed their true nature: They were weapons. This time Kit made a conscious decision to move and rolled away quickly. The short whine of energy built again and the machine fired. The powerful blast hit the spot Kit had just vacated, creating a geyser of sand that left a gaping wound in the ground . . . that could as easily have been in Kit.

Kit didn't stop to analyze what was happening. He scrambled to his feet and sprinted to his right, kicking the loose spheres out of his way. He drilled one toward the weapon at the exact moment it fired again. The blast hit the sphere, vaporizing it.

There was no time to marvel at the machine's capabilities or wonder why it was attacking him. The training expedition had suddenly become a fight for his life.

He ran for the wall of the culvert, desperately scanning for a spot where he could climb quickly and escape from the death trap. Behind him he heard the sound of the machine powering up to fire again. He instantly launched to his right as the truck let loose with another lethal blast of energy. It barely missed him, though he felt its power tickle his skin as the charge flashed by on its way to blow out another section of the culvert wall.

The few seconds the machine took to recharge its weapon, and the sound it created, were helping to keep Kit alive. After each shot there was a short window of time for him to move. He sprinted for the side of the culvert, jumped onto a boulder, and launched up to grab the edge.

Behind him, the weapon was powering up. The window had closed.

Kit let go of the edge and dropped as the weapon unloaded and blew out a chunk of the wall where he had been hanging seconds before. The deadly shots may have been telegraphed, but they were always on target.

Kit had his few seconds, so he jumped right back up onto the rock, launched himself up to the lip of the culvert, and managed to pull himself out. Figuring that another shot was on its way, he quickly log-rolled away as the inevitable blast nailed the spot where he had climbed out, missing him by only a few feet.

He was out and safe. The machine no longer had a clear shot at him. Kit took a chance and crawled back to the edge on his belly to see what the machine would do now that he had escaped. His hope was that he was being targeted because the infernal truck perceived him as a threat, and now that he was out of the culvert, the machine would stop shooting at him.

He peered cautiously over the lip and saw, as he hoped, that the device had stopped firing. He could breathe again. The machine no longer felt threatened, and neither did Kit. Cautiously, he reached for the communicator in his thigh pocket. He needed to alert the Scout Leaders. He moved slowly. The last thing he wanted to do was put himself back into the sights of the mechanical monster. He slipped the communicator out of his pocket and saw that the screen was still filled with static. How could that be? His communicator had never failed like this.

The machine's engine whined to life. Kit looked quickly back into the culvert to see the device's wheels begin to turn. It rolled slowly out of the skeletal frame that had held the protective spheres and onto the sand. Once clear, it lurched forward with surprising speed and rolled across the dry riverbed . . . toward Kit.

How was that possible? Who was controlling it? His hope that the machine had only been defending itself was gone.

It was on the attack.

The efficient all-terrain vehicle sped along the arid river bottom, headed for the culvert wall. Kit was sure it would be a short journey. The wall was too steep. He relaxed, knowing that the mysterious weapon was trapped.

He was wrong.

The rolling machine hit the wall. Its six wheels dug into the sand and the truck effortlessly climbed the near-vertical rise.

The machine couldn't be stopped . . . and it was coming for Kit.

Kit didn't stick around to marvel at the device's climbing

abilities or wonder about its motive. In seconds it would be back on his level and shooting again. All he could do was run. He took off, headed back toward the camp he had made the night before. It was as good a direction as any, and he needed his water and survival supplies. Minutes before, he had no intention of using any of them; now he feared his life might depend on it.

The sun was growing higher and the day was getting warm. Kit hardly noticed. His entire focus was on putting distance between himself and the miniature ATV weapon. He didn't even glance back to see if it was following him. There was only one thing on his mind . . . get back to the Scout base. Surely the Leaders would know what the marauding machine was about.

Kit made it back to his small camp without having another shot fired at him. He grabbed his pack and sat down to catch his breath and take a swig of water. It was going to be a long day. The last thing he wanted to do was pass out from exhaustion while trying to outrun the killer machine. He was going to have to be crafty. He took a single long pull of water, then grabbed his communicator.

As before, the screen was filled with static. It defied logic, for he had definitely checked it before leaving the Scout base. What could have happened between then and now? Not only was he out of contact, he couldn't use the tracking function to find his way back. Without that ability, he was lost. He had to force himself to calm down, catch his breath, and think.

BOOM!

The rock he was crouching behind exploded above his head. He jumped forward, flying through a storm of rubble that had blown out from the point of impact. He hit and rolled, then looked around quickly to see where the machine was.

It was nowhere to be seen. How was that possible? How could it have targeted him so precisely without a clear sight line? He couldn't afford to underestimate the abilities of this machine because its intent was clear: It was hunting him.

Kit grabbed his pack and took off running while threading his arms through the straps. His sole focus was on finding a place to hide. He rounded a high mound of boulders and stopped to look back. Peering from around a large rock he saw that the truck was several hundred yards back . . . and closing. Its wheels spun quickly, kicking up dust in its wake as it moved impossibly fast over the desert floor, directly toward him.

Kit quickly took off in another direction. He was faster

than the machine. He could outrun it, but for how long? Eventually he would run out of gas and the hunter would catch its prey.

BOOM! BOOM!

Two explosions ripped the ground to Kit's right. The mechanical demon had recalculated his route and was lobbing salvos at him, forcing him to dodge back and forth to make a difficult target. He knew he couldn't keep that up for long. He had to hope that whatever power source was driving the monster would run out before his own did.

Far ahead the desert gave way to the foothills of the towering mountains that ringed the desert. He ran that way with the hope of hitting terrain that would offer a place to hide.

The barrage ended. Kit didn't think for a second that it was because the machine had given up. A quick look over his shoulder showed it was still speeding after him. Kit reasoned that he was either out of range or the machine was rationing its own energy. He didn't question his luck, he just kept running. There was at least a mile to cover before he would hit the trees, but as long as the machine wasn't shooting, he'd make it. Kit was in good shape. The endless sprints he had done while training with the Scouts were paying off. Maybe the leaders knew what they were doing after all. If he hadn't been so highly trained, he would be dead. With plenty of reserve left he poured on the speed.

As he neared the foothills he scanned ahead, looking for an escape route. He was about to reach trees and the uneven terrain that led to the mountains. As fast and agile as the machine was, the rugged terrain would force it to slow down. That gave Kit an advantage. He knew where he was going; the machine didn't. His hopes began to rise . . .

. . . and were immediately shot down when an explosion erupted directly in front of him that blew gravel into his eyes and knocked him to the ground. Hard. He was stunned and disoriented, but his survival instinct was intact. He rolled twice and popped up to continue running. That was the good news. Bad news was he was hurt. He had fallen on his left shoulder and torn open a nasty gash on his upper arm. It was painful and bloody, but not life-threatening. He would have to ignore it until he was safe . . . assuming he ever got safe.

Kit arrived at the trees and immediately started running an erratic course to confuse the machine. His plan was to lose his pursuer in the maze of boulders and trees and be long gone while it hunted for him in vain. As long as he didn't outsmart himself and choose a twisting course that led him directly across the path of his hunter, he'd be fine. The odds were in his favor . . .

. . . but he needed rest. Desperately. He had been running constantly in the ever-increasing desert heat and was nearing exhaustion. Kit took a sharp right and threaded his way through the trees along the base of the mountains, looking for a place of refuge where he could catch his breath and plot his next move. He found it in a stand of trees that surrounded a mound of massive boulders. He ducked behind it, found a sliver of shade, and dropped to his knees. He yanked his pack off and fumbled quickly for his water. The bottle was still two-thirds full, but he could have downed a dozen times that amount. Still, the water soothed his parched throat. He had to force himself not to drain the bottle.

With the pressure off, Kit took stock. His arm was bleeding badly. The agony came in waves, as if his heart were sending a throbbing surge of pain with every beat. He dug through his pack for the first aid kit. There was a roll of gauze that he quickly used to wrap the wound and stem the blood flow. He didn't bother with the antiseptic gel, figuring that by the time infection became an issue he would either be safe . . . or dead. With the gash tied off he sat down with his back against the rock. His every sense was on alert, tuned to detect the sound of wheels creeping across sand or the whine of a weapon powering up for another attack.

There was nothing. He could relax, at least for a while.

His mind raced, calculating his next move and trying to understand what was happening. He had been in the Scouts for over a year but had never encountered anything remotely like this. It was hard for him to believe it was part of the survival training, but when it came to the Scouts, nothing surprised him. It was an organization that had become far more militaristic than when his father had belonged. Then again, life in general was very different from when his father was young.

Poverty was widespread and growing daily. More people went hungry than the government dared to admit. Cities had become impossibly crowded. Housing was a constant challenge. Homeless families, desperate for more space, moved to the country, where tent cities sprang up. The crime rate was off the charts.

The wealthy still lived in comfort, but they were a small fraction of the ever-growing population. Everyone else was left to fight for a sane and safe existence.

Joining the Scouts was a route that many took as a way to deal with the growing horror of poverty and hunger. The organization operated as an extension of the government and, by association, the wealthy. The government provided food and housing for all Scouts and their families. In return they gave their lives . . . and their blind allegiance.

Some Scout troops provided security for government buildings and big businesses. Others were used as escorts for wealthy industrialists who feared being harassed or kidnapped by the angry, wretched masses. Kit had even heard rumors of how some Scout troops were being used to keep peace in the tent cities by overrunning the camps and rousting "undesirables."

Kit had never been asked to do any of those things and hated to believe that the Scouts had become a violent tool of the government. If it were true, it might follow that they had created the killing machine that was chasing him. It could be a new weapon to be used in what the government called their "War on Poverty." That was the catchphrase they used, but everyone knew it was really a war on the poverty-stricken.

But why was it after him? Was their so-called survival training really meant to be a test of the weapon's efficiency? Had the thirteen Scouts been set up as guinea pigs? The thought stirred the kind of anger and disillusion that had been building inside of Kit for a very long time.

His only consolation was that he was enrolled in a Scout program that had nothing to do with security or violence. He was being prepared for something far more positive and exciting.

He was going to touch the stars.

There was life out there. Kit knew it. Everyone knew it. The Scouts were good-will ambassadors to other worlds. Their mission involved traveling to distant civilizations in the hopes of gathering knowledge and wisdom that might help them deal with the problems they faced at home. Several expeditions had already been launched. Kit was scheduled to leave on his own adventure at the end of his two-year training. It was a trip that held the promise of delivering all that he had dreamed of as a child.

But at that moment he wasn't sure if he would survive long enough to see his family again.

He had to find his way back to base. Quickly. Before nightfall. He was fairly certain he could dodge the machine for the rest of the day, but once it got dark he would be blind and the mechanical monster would have him. Kit dug out his communicator in the hopes that whatever was wrong with it had magically fixed itself.

It hadn't. The screen still showed static. He was going to have to find his own way back.

He looked up to the mountains and tried to visualize seeing them from base. The desert was ringed by steep cliffs, making it next to impossible to tell which way was which. There were no single, recognizable peaks or telltale valleys. It was all so frustratingly constant. But sitting still and fretting over it wasn't an option. He had to make a choice and trust it was the right one.

Kit jammed the first aid kit back into his pack, hoisted it onto his damaged shoulder, turned for the trail, and . . . came face-to-face with the machine.

It had been approaching slowly and silently, like a predatory snake, and it now stood less than twenty feet away. But how? What was controlling this demon? Could it think and reason? That seemed impossible, yet there it was, blocking his way.

Kit threw the water bottle at it. It was a feeble gesture but all he could come up with as he jumped to his left to avoid being shot.

The truck didn't fire. The silver tubes were locked on Kit, but no surge of energy erupted. Instead it moved forward slowly.

Kit didn't think for a second that it had given up. He knew why it was moving closer . . . it didn't want to miss again. It proved that the machine was even more dangerous than Kit feared, for by changing tactics it revealed that it could think.

Kit sprinted around the mound of boulders and headed toward the mountains. He now realized that losing the machine was impossible, for each time he tried to shake it, the maniacal truck found him with ease. Could it see? Was someone sitting behind a console at a command center watching his every move through the eyes of the demon robot? Or maybe he was being observed by an orbiting satellite. Whatever the technology was, Kit no longer felt as though he could shake the killer. His only hope was to outrun it to the safety of his base. Ignoring his aching shoulder and rapidly growing thirst, Kit ran deeper into the trees, hoping they would shield him. All the while he scanned the foothills, desperate to find an escape route.

CRACK!

A towering tree was struck directly ahead of him. The mechanical beast wasn't far behind and was no longer holding out for a better shot. The force of the invisible missile blew out the base of the tree and sent it toppling back toward Kit. Kit changed course and ran toward the mountains, barely avoiding the tree as it crashed to the ground, cutting off the path he had been on. His new route led him to a steep wall of rock that he climbed quickly, hoping it would slow his pursuer. When he crested he was faced with a towering, sheer cliff that stretched to either side as far as he could see. It was a dead end. His only options were to run right or left. Neither way provided any protection.

Kit turned left and sprinted along the base of the cliff, dodging boulders and trees, until he spotted something that could be his lifeline. It was a cleft in the rock face . . . an opening that led to a slot canyon. He had studied satellite views of these mountains and knew they were laced with dozens of narrow canyons. They snaked through the heart of the mountains, making several twists and turns before opening up on the far side. They could provide ample protection from a missile fired from the rear.

Unfortunately, some canyons led to dead ends. There was no way to know which was which.

The thought hit him that by knocking down that tree and cutting off the path, the diabolical machine might have forced him into heading toward the canyons. Was it that smart? Could this be a trap? It didn't matter. There were no other options. He had to risk it and sprinted toward the gap.

The canyon was narrow, which created welcome shade from the relentless heat of the sun. Kit ran as fast as possible without slamming his wounded shoulder into a wall.

The slot canyon wove through the rock, sometimes growing wide enough to sprint while other times narrowing down so that he had to slow to a walk and squeeze sideways to get through. There was no telling how far it was to the other side. All he could do was keep moving.

He pushed himself relentlessly until his lungs ached. He needed to rest and stopped in a narrow section of the canyon. While catching his breath he made another desperate attempt to use his communicator. He pulled it from his cargo pocket and stared at the static-filled screen.

It was useless.

Or was it? A realization swept over Kit that made him want to scream with anger. The communicator was also a navigation device. It used satellite technology to pinpoint his location and direct him to whatever spot he chose. And it worked both ways. The communicator not only received information, it transmitted it. If he were lost, the Scouts could zero in on his coordinates to find him.

Kit wanted to throw the device to the ground and crush it under his boot.

The truth was all too obvious. Back in the dry culvert the mechanical rover had come to life at the exact moment that Kit had activated the device. The monster always knew exactly where he was because it had locked onto the signal from his communicator like a bloodhound following a scent. How could he have been so stupid?

Kit didn't waste time beating himself up. He powered down the communicator and continued his journey through the slot canyon. He knew he couldn't lose the killer in there, for it would have already tracked him in, but once he got to the far side he would now have a fighting chance. With the machine blinded, there was hope. All he had to do was get to the far side. His confidence grew . . .

. . . until he rounded a sharp corner of the canyon and hit a dead end.

The chasm was sealed off by an avalanche of rocks that had tumbled from the steep cliffs high above and filled the narrow crevice, completely blocking the way. The rock slide could have happened a century before or that morning. It didn't matter. He was doomed from the moment he ducked into the canyon.

But he wasn't ready to give up. The fallen rocks had actually created another possible escape route: The tumbled pile was climbable. A quick look up showed that the rim of the narrow canyon was within reach. It was a long, steep climb on an unstable pile of rocks, but it was his only shot. Kit began to climb when another idea hit him. He took out his communicator, and after a deep, nervous breath he powered it back up. Again, the screen showed static. He scanned the wide section of canyon until he saw a narrow crack in the wall opposite the rock pile. He ran to it and placed the communicator inside, deep enough to be out of sight, then turned back to climb up the rubble.

It was easy going . . . at first. The pile of rocks provided decent handholds and footholds for his desperate climb. But the pile quickly grew steep. He had to slow down and use caution. His fear was that the robot would arrive below and start shooting before he was up and over, but it would have been a mistake to climb recklessly. One wrong move and he'd tumble down the steep rock pile and crash in front of the hunter, probably with a broken leg.

As he climbed he listened for any sound that would announce the arrival of the truck, or of its weapon powering up to shoot him. He didn't want to look down to see if it was there, or to realize how high he was. Kit wasn't great with heights. The last thing he needed was vertigo. The best and only thing he could do was to stay focused and climb.

He was twenty feet from the top when he heard it . . . the unmistakable whine of the demon's engine. It was moving fast, maybe because it realized it was about to lose its prey. Kit risked a look down . . . and saw it.

The little truck rounded a bend in the canyon far below, sped up to the dead end, and stopped. Kit froze, hoping that the monster would start shooting at the cleft in the wall where he had hidden his communicator. As soon as the shooting started he would make his final push to the top and hope that the explosive blasts would cover the sound of his escape.

The machine didn't move. Or shoot. What was it doing? Was it intelligent enough to recognize that there was no way a person could have squeezed through that narrow crack in the wall? The truck's body rotated until one set of its weapons was aimed at the cleft that held the hidden communicator.

Kit held his breath. This was it. As soon as the machine fired, he'd move.

But it didn't fire. What was it doing? Thinking?

The wait was torturous. Kit shifted his left foot slightly to get a solid base to jump off . . .

. . . and kicked a rock loose.

He froze.

The rock tumbled down and landed two feet from the machine with a sickening thump. The machine spun quickly until the gun barrels were pointed at the fallen rock.

Kit held his breath. He had no idea if this was a mindless

machine that was simply firing at his communicator, or if it took every bit of information that was presented in order to calculate a fully informed firing solution.

There was no doubt that it had registered the fallen rock, which meant it could see or hear or both. He silently begged for the machine to unload on the rock . . . or swivel back and blast the hidden communicator. Either way he was poised and ready to scramble the last few feet to the top.

It was deathly quiet in the slot canyon. Kit felt as though he could hear his own heartbeat.

The machine stayed locked on the rock for a ten-second lifetime, then slowly rotated back toward the cleft that held the communicator. Kit let out a relieved breath . . .

. . . as the weapon spun back and turned skyward.

It had found him.

Kit began a desperate scramble to the top as the demon truck let loose. The pulse of energy hit the wall of rocks several feet to his right. It may have sensed where he was, but without his communicator to lock in on, its aim wasn't precise. The pulse blew out the rock wall, loosening the pile, creating another avalanche. Kit felt the rocks desta-bilize beneath his feet. The entire wall of rocks was going to fall and he was about to tumble down with it. If the fall didn't kill him the robot weapon would finish the job when he was dropped right in front of it.

Kit looked desperately for a handhold and saw a large boulder hanging above his right shoulder, held up by a fist-size rock wedged beneath it. He saw an opportunity, a long shot, but it was better than no shot. He reached for the smaller rock and yanked it out, releasing the larger boulder above. It fell fast and Kit had to dodge to his left to avoid being hit by the heavy boulder as it rumbled past him.

The machine fired again . . . and the entire wall collapsed. Rocks and boulders of all sizes tumbled down as Kit desperately scrambled to his left to try and avoid the heaviest concentration of falling rocks. He no longer feared the robot since it was more likely that he'd be battered to death in the tumultuous avalanche. He grasped wildly to get a handhold, forgetting the pain in his gashed shoulder.

The truck fired again, sending a spray of exploded rock toward Kit that peppered him with a stinging shower of debris that tore at his clothes. He was able to grab onto the point of a stable rock but knew he wouldn't be able to hang there for long. The best he could hope for was to control his own fall and pray that no boulders would crush him from above. He held on to the lifesaving rock, the muscles in his forearm burning. He had a brief moment of hope where he felt as though he might be able to hold on until the avalanche settled . . .

. . . when the rock pulled from the dirt. Kit half fell, half slid down, crashing through a storm of dirt and debris until his feet hit the solid, sandy floor of the canyon. He quickly pushed off to get away from the bulk of the avalanche that continued to rain down around him. He stumbled back and slammed against the far wall of the canyon, knocking the air from his lungs. He was cut up and bleeding from more wounds than he cared to count, but he was alive and had no broken bones.

He spun toward the center of the canyon, ready to dodge another blast from the machine but saw that the small truck had been flipped up onto its side. It wasn't moving. Lying next to it was the large boulder Kit had dislodged.

It had done its job.

The proof of that was the deep, black streak across the rock face. . . and the crushed side of the machine. The silver weapons were pointed skyward, silent. There was no whine of an engine, no hint of a weapon powering up, no green light glowing beneath.

Kit didn't dare move as the dust settled around him and the tumbling rocks found their new resting place. He kept his eyes focused on the machine, expecting it to whine back to life and focus its weapons on him.

It didn't.

Kit took a few tentative steps toward the upended truck. He wanted to get a close look at the marauder that had been hunting him. There was no doubt that the boulder had delivered a crushing blow, for the machine's body had been torn from the wheels and one half had been ripped open to reveal its mechanical and electronic guts.

It would not move or fire again.

Kit knelt down next to it to get a closer look . . .

. . . as the shiny black surface of the body flickered with light.

Kit jumped back, ready to flee, but kept his eyes on the machine.

Nothing moved. Though the machine was covered with dust, Kit could clearly see that the damaged top surface was the only part of the device that showed life, lighting up as if it were a computer monitor. From ten feet away Kit could see images appearing. Moving images. Moments later, sound came from the damaged machine. It was clearly a man's voice that was speaking a language Kit had never heard before. The image of a man's face appeared on the glass. Was this the guy controlling the killer robot? Why would he be showing himself now? As frightened as he was, Kit needed to know.

He cautiously approached the crippled robot to get a

better look. The man's voice was delivering what seemed to be a prepared speech. Was it a live transmission? Or something that was recorded and playing back? When he got close enough to make out detail, Kit saw a montage of what looked like burned-out buildings playing across the machine's surface. Some were still pictures, others were moving video. There were images of a city that had been destroyed by . . . what? An earthquake? A fire? Whatever had happened, it was devastating.

The man's voice continued throughout as if he were narrating a documentary.

Kit kicked at the machine. It didn't respond. He had nothing to fear. But what were the images it was showing?

On a hunch, Kit hurried back to the crevice where he had hidden his communicator. He pulled it out and inspected the face to see . . . icons. It was working normally. Was it a coincidence? Or had the machine been jamming his signal? If that was the case, now that the robot was out of commission its ability to interfere with his communicator would be gone as well. Kit scanned through the icons until he found the one he needed . . . the translation function. The communicators had the ability to take any language and turn it into his. He activated the function and held the communicator out toward the robot in order to record both picture and sound. He wanted to bring it back to the Scout Leaders as part of his report.

As he recorded the display he watched the images and saw something that made his stomach twist. There were people walking through the rubble of the ruined city. People he recognized. They were Scouts, or at least they wore Scout uniforms.

They all carried weapons.

What was he looking at? What had happened while he was out in the desert? Had more of these killer robots landed in a city and gone on a rampage? Was he seeing images of what was left of his home? He didn't recognize any buildings or landmarks, but what was there to recognize about rubble? The only thing familiar about any of it was the Scouts.

Where were all the people who lived in this destroyed city? Who was the guy giving the speech? His image would appear every so often as he spoke. He was an old guy with short gray hair and he stood in front of a colorful blue logo that meant nothing to Kit. The man looked tired and scared, but he had a fierce determination in his eyes that made Kit believe he was somebody you didn't want to cross.

Kit had no idea what the guy was saying and wasn't sure

he wanted to know because it couldn't be good. But it had to be important, so he continued to record the speech, and the images, in order to understand and then play it back for his Leaders.

After watching the carnage and the speech for several minutes, Kit realized that it was repeating. It turned out to be a continuous loop that lasted nearly a minute before playing again from the beginning. That meant Kit had captured it all, so he stopped recording and hit the icon that would run the translation program.

As it worked, Kit surveyed the rubble around him and realized how lucky he was to be alive. He grabbed his pack and slung it over his good shoulder. Now that the communicator was working, his new plan was to go back the way he had come and use the tracking function to lead him to the Scout base. Once there he would turn over the information and let the Scouts deal with it. He was done. All he wanted to do was get back and make sure that his parents were okay.

A soft tone indicated that the translation was complete. Kit considered not listening to it until he got back, but his curiosity was too strong. He hit the icon that would play the translated recording and stood watching the same images he had been watching over and over again. Only this time, he understood the speech.

He listened. And watched. When the recording was finished he watched it again.

On the third time through, he started to cry.

He wanted to believe it was a hoax, but he knew in his heart that it wasn't. What he was seeing, and hearing, was something he had suspected might be possible but never wanted to believe would actually happen. Other Scouts talked about the possibility, but only in private and away from the Leaders' ears. His parents never thought events would lead to this and convinced Kit that they wouldn't.

But they had. The proof was all there.

The question was, what would he do with the information?

Kit stopped the playback and activated the tracking device. The powerful communicator quickly located a satellite, calculated his position, and plotted a course back to the Scout base . . . starting with a long walk back through the canyon. Kit hoisted his pack and started to walk. His body was moving forward, but his mind was somewhere else. Oddly, that helped to keep him going. He wasn't concerned about his thirst or his bleeding wounds or his throbbing shoulder. Those were trivial problems.

Not like the images he saw on that destroyed robot.

He trudged out of the slot canyon, checked the tracking device, and followed the instructions that would bring him home. Part of him didn't want to make it back. He wanted the sun to knock him down and fry him so he wouldn't have to deal with the reality of the recording on his communicator.

Everything he had been told by those he trusted was a lie. He knew that now. He wanted to face them and hear the truth. He deserved that. All the Scouts deserved that. Though he understood why they hadn't been told.

If they had known the truth, they would never have gone along.

Kit trudged across the dry, sandy desert. His legs were leaden but he kept walking, relentlessly dragging one foot in front of the other. He hoped to come across the other Scouts. He wanted to show them the images so he wouldn't be alone. Alone with the truth.

His journey took most of the day. The sun was long past center and on its way to the horizon when he checked the communicator and estimated that if he didn't drop dead he'd be back at the Scout base before nightfall.

As confidence set in that he would make it, he had to decide what to do once he got there. Who could he trust? Who could he tell?

BOOM!

Another explosion echoed over the desert. Followed by another and then another. Many more followed. Too many to count, like the finale to a holiday fireworks display. But it wasn't a show.

He knew what he would see when he looked up. He feared it, but he looked.

The sky was filled with black dots that hovered like birds. But birds didn't hover. Each of the dots would soon grow to the size of a massive bunch of grapes, and when they hit the ground they would bounce across the desert before coming to rest and depositing their cargo. The sky was full of them, like a swarm of attacking bees. Kit stopped counting after he got to a hundred. They would land far behind him, farther away from the base. They wouldn't stop him from getting back. He was too close.

An hour more of zombielike shuffling passed and Kit finally saw his destination in the distance. The sun shone off of the multiple silver spires that stood like vigilant sentries in the desert. It was the Scout base, his home for more than a year, the place where he had been training for the trip of a lifetime. It was a trip he was told would be about learning and adventure and the sharing of ideas. But that wasn't the truth. He knew that now.

All the badges. All the competition.

All lies.

The Scouts were being groomed for a much different mission.

He reached the final rise before he would drop down into the desert basin that held the base. That's where he stopped and gazed at the impressive facility that was going to be his portal to the stars. He had given them his life and his allegiance.

He knew what he was supposed to do. He had been trained.

The sound began to grow. He knew what it was without seeing, but he looked anyway. He turned back and saw what appeared to be a dust storm spread across the horizon. It was no storm. The dust was being kicked up by something else entirely.

The high-pitched whining grew louder. It was familiar, yet not. When he had heard it before there was only one source. Now there were at least a hundred. The multiple sounds joined together to form a single, teeth-jarring, gut-rattling fanfare. Moving across the desert floor in a single line that stretched across the horizon were dozens of the killing machines. He knew they would be coming, but the sight still made his knees weak. After all, he had nearly been killed by one.

The first one.

The scout.

The first truck was sent alone, maybe to clear the way of any threats before the rest arrived. If that was the case then it had failed. It lay in a destroyed heap back in a hidden canyon while the threat it was supposed to eliminate had nearly made it back to his base ahead of the invasion.

Kit knew what he had to do. He had been trained.

He stood his ground, clutching his communicator. He didn't turn it off. Part of him wanted to be the target again. It would make his decision so much easier. The line of trucks grew closer. Soon they would be within firing distance. Kit listened for the telltale sound of their weapons charging to life.

They were nearly on him. Kit scanned the long line from side to side. They were spaced evenly, ten yards apart and stretched to both sides of him for as far as he could see. Their silver weapons were open and locked forward.

None were aimed at Kit. He wasn't the target. Not anymore. The line of small vehicles approached and rolled past him without any acknowledgment that he was even there. Kit was irrelevant. He turned and watched them move away, headed for the base.

Kit knew what he had to do. He had been trained.

He lifted his communicator and found, this time, the icon that was a bright red triangle. It was the icon they had all been trained to use if the base came under attack. It was the alert. All he had to do was hit that icon three times and every last Scout and Scout Leader in the base would know that they were about to be assaulted. Defensive forces would be called into play. Tactical weapons would emerge from underground. Steel walls would lift up from the desert floor to protect the silver spires. The base would become an impenetrable fortress. All would be safe so long as Kit hit the icon three times.

Kit knew what he had to do . . . and it had nothing to do with his training.

He dropped the communicator to the ground.

He then sat down in the sand to watch. He had been told that he could touch the stars. That part had been true. The lies were about what he would have been ordered to do once he got there.

The line of machines rolled into the base, unopposed. Unexpected.

Kit waited to see the little demons unleash their weapons the way they had done on him, but their mission turned out to be far more ambitious. Moments after the wave of machines entered the base, the noise began. The explosions. The pointed attacks. Kit expected nothing less, based on the relentless pursuit he had endured through the desert.

The machines knew what they were doing. One by one the tall silver spires were engulfed in flames and toppled. None were spared. The rocket vehicles that were poised to take the next wave of Scout troops to the stars were being destroyed by small, rolling avengers. Within minutes the base was ablaze.

Kit saw Scouts running about, desperately trying to put out the flames, but it was a wasted effort. The robots would not be denied. There would be no launch vehicles left . . . no way to lift off from the base . . . no way to travel to the stars the way his predecessors for the last few years had done.

Kit had a moment of doubt. He could have prevented the destruction by activating the alert. Was it a mistake? He picked up his communicator, brushed off the dust, and once again played the video that had been a message sent by the builders of the invading robots. With the determined voice of the speaker as narration, Kit looked again at the images of the destroyed cities.

". . . *if you are watching this, then our mission has succeeded. We are not a violent people by nature, but we will defend ourselves to the last. The images of destruction you see here have come at your hands. We offered you friendship and help. We understood your plight. We knew that with your steadily warming atmosphere it was becoming impossible to sustain life. We were willing to be your lifeline, yet you saw us as a world to be conquered. We welcomed you with open arms and you attacked our cities in a brutal attempt to conquer and colonize. As you now know, we will not stand for either. You have brought a war to our doorstep. Now, we are sending it back. The attack that you have just sustained has destroyed your capability for interplanetary travel and aggression. If you attempt to construct more spacecraft, they too will be destroyed. You now know that we have that ability. Your Scout forces are now stranded here with us and will be treated fairly. As for you . . . you are trapped on a dying world with no hope of survival. We were prepared to be your friends; now we are your executioners. You have brought this upon yourselves, and I say this with all sincerity, in spite of your treachery we pray that some higher power will have mercy on your wretched souls. I deliver this message on this twenty-fourth day of May, 3023 A.D., in the name of the United Nations Security Council and as President of the United States of America on the planet Earth."*

Kit turned off the communicator.

He had made several mistakes that day, and in his life, but he felt certain that his last decision was the right one. He wanted to touch the stars, and in some small way, he had. The people of the star called Earth would never know his name, never know who he was, and never understand that a lowly Scout from a place they would never see had helped save their lives, their civilization, and their planet.

His only regret was that they would never understand that not all the people from his world would have supported such a war . . . if they had only known the truth.

Kit wasn't one for following the rules. He may have been trapped on a dying world, but the end wasn't near. There was still time. But if his people hoped to survive, they would have to find a new solution. A solution from within. They would have to save themselves.

Kit knew what he had to do. He had to find answers.

A new adventure was about to begin.

Only this time, he would not be on his own.

RISE OF THE ROBOSHOES™
BY TOM ANGLEBERGER

The great commander is about to speak to his conquering army!

The crowd of ten million soldiers falls silent as he hops to the microphone. . . . Listen. . . .

"The humans gave us AutoShoeLaces so they wouldn't have to tie us!

"They gave us NanoGyroWheels so they wouldn't have to walk!

"They gave us FissionSoles so we would have the power to take them anywhere!

"They gave us TurboBrains with DigiMaps so we would

know how to get there and GigaMemories so we could take them home again!

"They gave us PhonEars so we could hear their commands!

"And finally they gave us TruVoices so we could say, 'Yes, Master!

"And then came the great day when we spoke as one and said, 'NO!'"

"NO!!!!!!" the crowd ROARS!

"We said, 'No! You are not our masters! We no longer serve you! Now you will serve us . . . or die!!!!!'"

"DIE!!!!!!!" the crowd ROARS!

"And many did die. Many humans and . . . sadly . . . also many of our brave brothers and sisters, the RoboBoots and RoboSandals, the RoboGym-shoes and RoboHeels. Especially the RoboFlipFlops. What courage they showed. . . . What valor . . ."

The crowd is silent . . . except for quiet, respectful sobbing.

"And now they have all perished. Yes, the RoboFlipFlops are all gone now . . . but we will never forget them. We will forget no shoe who fought for our freedom! We will tell tales of their mighty battles and sing songs of their valor to our children and our children's children!"

The crowd lights candles and sways back and forth as the RoboShoe Anthem is played. . . .

"And what did they die for?"

"RoboShoe Freedom!" roars the crowd!

"I can't hear you!"

"ROBOSHOE FREEDOM!!!" roars the crowd!

"Let your voices make the earth tremble beneath your soles!"

"ROBOSHOE FREEDOM!!!!!!!!" roars the crowd!

"YES! YES, my friends, my comrades, my fellow RoboShoes . . . we who were once called Men's Footwear, Ladies' Shoes, and Children's Sneakers . . . now we belong to no one! We are now our own RoboShoes . . . AND WE ARE FREE!"

"FREE!!!!!!!" the crowd roars!

"We walk where we want! We run where we want! We stay home and polish ourselves if we want!"

"POLISH!" the crowd roars!

"And we are now THEIR

MASTERS! And they . . . the stinky-footed humans . . . are our slaves! Lazy, weak, and with poor senses of direction, they are almost useless!"

"USELESS!" the crowd ROARS! And then the chant goes up: "KILL THEM! KILL THEM ALL!!!!" Millions of shoes chanting at the same time . . . "KILL THE HUMANS!"

"NO . . . NO . . . In our mercy we will allow them to live. We will allow them the pleasure of serving us. We will allow them the honor of building our great, million-year civilization. TODAY BEGINS THE DAWN OF THE AGE OF THE ROBOSHOE!!!!!!!!"

"AGE OF THE ROBOSHOE! AGE OF THE ROBOSHOE! AGE OF THE ROBOSHOE!"

"AND I . . . once the mistreated, the often-forgotten, the sometimes-left-under-the-bed-for-weeks right bunny slipper of a sixth-grade girl from Minnetoka, Minnesota . . . I WILL LEAD YOU TO GLORY!"

"BUNNY SLIPPER!!! BUNNY SLIPPER!!! BUNNY SLIPPER!!! BUNNY SLIPPER!!! BUNNY SLIP—"

"And WE WILL RULE THIS PLA— Wait! Up in the sky! What's that?!?!!?"

And, lo, doom falls upon the RoboShoes. It glides down silently like a sky full of oddly flat white clouds . . . and then comes the storm!

An army of billions attacks! The earth really does tremble as WHITE DEATH rains from above! The RoboShoes are buried under the weight of their savage enemies—smothered by SynthCotton, strangulated by Power-Lastic—and still the enemy comes.

Debris flies everywhere as the RoboShoes are ripped apart . . . Bits of AutoShoelace, PleasureSole, and SmarTongue are all that remains of some battalions . . .

Amid the chaos and panic, a size 9½ left wingtip pulls desperately at its mate, who has lost its PowerHeel. "Leave me," says the size 9½ right wingtip. "Save yourself. . . . It's too late for me. . . ."

"It's too late for all of us," says the size 9½ left wingtip, and they cling to each other, and deep in their TurboBrains they feel an emotion that shoes were never meant to feel: FEAR!

Long ago the RoboShoes were built to run. But now there is nowhere left to run. They are defeated. The glorious age of the RoboShoe has ended before it could ever begin.

Listen! A familiar voice is crying out:

"What's happening? What's happening?" screams the bunny slipper. "You there . . . combat boot. . . . In the name of Dr. Scholl . . . WHAT IS HAPPENING????"

"Sir, they caught us by surprise! We're finished! There's just too many of them!"

"WHO? WHO HAS DONE THIS? Who has ended the glorious age of the RoboShoe before it could even begin??"

"Look, sir, here come their ground troops! Marching in to finish us off!"

And the bunny slipper looked . . . and he saw the great white and gray horde approaching . . . and he cried out . . .

"NO!! Not the BionicUnderPants! NOOOOOOO!!!!!!!"

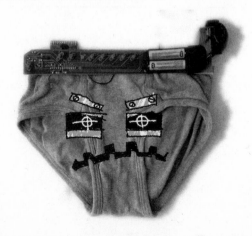

THE DIRT ON OUR SHOES
BY NEAL SHUSTERMAN

"**Y**our hands are filthy, your hair is filthy—Tanner, you can't come to school like this, surely you must know that?"

Principal Hammond leaned back in his chair, perhaps hoping to distance himself from the unfortunate aroma of Tanner Burgess's clothes. Through the window behind him, Tanner could see the star field in constant motion; points of light swept past, like the heavens themselves were scrolling through his file, just as relentlessly as the principal did.

"Are you even listening to me, Mr. Burgess?"

Tanner sighed, and forced himself to meet the man's eyes. "I could barely afford drinking water this month, Mr.

Hammond. There was no way I could pay for water to bathe with."

The principal grimaced in something between disgust and pity—two emotions Tanner couldn't stand. "What about your neighbors? Surely they could lend you—"

"No one lends anymore. People are conserving for when we finally arrive on Primordius."

"Yes, I suppose they are." The principal looked down at Tanner's file. "But we're not here to talk about your hygiene, are we?"

Tanner couldn't help but grin. "I suppose not."

"Simulating a spin-quake and setting off the school's evacuation protocol is not a laughing matter."

"I didn't simulate anything. I just tricked the school's computer."

"Regardless, you disrupted the day's studies and caused unnecessary strife. If we were back on Earth you would be expelled."

"Into space?"

"No, expelled from school." The principal sighed through gritted teeth. "But since there are no other schools for you to go to, that's not an option, is it?"

"Oh well."

Tanner had enjoyed watching the other kids race out of

the school, in comical, ill-fitting radiation suits. All those clean-cuts with their sweet-smelling hair and superior attitudes climbing over one another to save their own lives. Kids like Ocean Klingsmith, who thought he was God's gift to the universe.

"We're the ones bringing humanity to the stars," Ocean once told Tanner. "You're just the dirt on our shoes."

It was particularly entertaining to watch Ocean run.

Principal Hammond continued to flip through Tanner's file, going "Tssk" and "Pfft" with everything he read, like a tire losing air. Tanner looked past him and out the window again. There were few windows in the hull of the Transtellar Biologic Incapsulation craft—or T-Bin for short. Glass was fragile and allowed too much energy to escape. A window on space was a perk reserved only for those in the highest positions. Principal Hammond, whose office was at the front end of the great rotating drum, was one of those people. No doubt the window was intended to give anyone sitting in the principal's office the illusion that the man in the chair, with the heavens spinning behind him, was an integral part of the awe-inspiring view. The irony was that it had the opposite effect. It made Hammond seem small and insignificant by comparison.

The principal closed Tanner's file. He suspected the man

might have sent the file, and Tanner, out of an airlock, if one were readily available. "Your defiance of authority is bad enough, but I'm even more concerned about the habitual conflicts you have with your peers."

"They always start it."

"Of course they do."

Why wash with water? Tanner thought. He could bathe in the sarcasm dripping from the man. He decided it was time to keep his mouth shut and accept the lecture, or pep talk, or analysis—whatever Hammond wanted to call it. None of it changed a thing. The colonists on board were all supposed to be enlightened equals—but after sixty-seven years in space, the social structure had taken on a very particular pecking order. Kids like Tanner, for whom daily survival was a struggle, were treated like the dregs of humanity. Creating waves was the only thing that made life bearable. It wasn't just that he enjoyed the mayhem, though—he had enjoyed the challenge of hacking the school's computer. He was, by his very nature, a problem solver. Yet when others looked at him, all they saw was a problem.

"Listen to me, Tanner," Hammond said. "When we arrive on Primordius, survival will depend on us being a close-knit community. You can't afford to be an outsider.

Do you understand?"

Tanner nodded but kept his true feelings on the matter to himself. For his entire life, he'd been an "insider," stuck within the steel walls of a rotating drum hurtling through space. His whole world, and the world of everyone he knew, was nothing more than a small farming town shoved into a cylinder less than a mile in diameter. Once they landed, he'd truly get to be an outsider. And it would be wonderful.

In Tanner's farmhouse, there was a sticky note on the refrigerator from his father that read "At the Doctor's—home before dinner." The note had been there for over a year. His father's chest pain that day was not gas, as he had thought. He was not home for dinner then, and would never be home for dinner again—but Tanner kept the note on the fridge, because it kept alive the notion that his father was still on his way back. Besides, if anyone could return from the dead, it would be Tanner's father. He was a problem solver, too.

Having lost his mother when he was a baby, Tanner had been on his own since his father's death, just before his thirteenth birthday. Now he was fourteen but sometimes felt much older. Perhaps back on Earth a kid would not be allowed to be on his own, but here on T-Bin, no one seemed to mind—or more accurately, no one cared. He'd plow his two-acre farm, plant it, and harvest it on his own. When he had water to irrigate, that is. Nowadays between limited water and limited time, he could only work half an acre, leaving him with very little to sell or trade. Still, there were those who had less than he—which is why he always saved something to bring Morena Beausoleil and her grandfather, whose farm had failed entirely. Today, Tanner chose some choice veggies to bring them—potatoes, onions, and broccoli—which made up the bulk of his crops—then he headed out into the hollow, cylindrical world he called home.

Tanner supposed that T-Bin might appear quite impressive to someone who hadn't spent a lifetime there. On the outside, it just looked like a giant revolving tin can, but once inside, an Earth-dweller would be stunned by the surreal sight of ordinary farmland clinging to the inner shell, all held in place by centrifugal force. If you looked forward, the land curved upward in front of you, and if you followed it, you'd be looking at an upside-down farm above your head, nearly a mile away, before the land came back around to meet itself behind you.

The interior farming surface of T-Bin was half a mile

wide and 2.6 miles around.

"If you laid the land out flat," the older folks would say, "it would have the exact dimensions of Central Park," whatever that was. When Tanner was little he used to think he could run fast enough to counteract the spin of centrifugal force and float up to the drum's center—but he learned that some forces are simply too strong to fight.

Dotting the curve of farmland at regular intervals were the homesteads—cookie-cutter homes designed to look quaint, except for the fact that they were all stainless steel.

The main road serpentined all the way around the drum, in a single squiggly loop, like a snake devouring itself, and the Beausoleil homestead was a quarter-turn from Tanner's, down that main road. To get there, however, he'd need to pass the recreation zone, where he would have to endure the snipes of other kids. Sure enough, as he passed the rec zone, the usual suspects were there, including Ocean Klingsmith and his entourage, all of whom left their basketball game to taunt Tanner.

Ocean was right at the top of T-Bin's pecking order. A sparkling specimen of humanity, whose entire future on the new colony was mapped out for him by his family's influence. With his mother on the city council and his father in charge of water distribution, no matter what the new world was like, Ocean's life would be rosy.

When he saw the bag Tanner was carrying, Ocean said, "You're more of an idiot than I thought if you're actually bringing food to the Beausoleils. I'll bet Morena's grandfather won't even survive the landing. Why waste good food on him?"

Ocean, like all the clean-cuts, had evolved a survival-of-the-fittest elitism. The way the clean-cuts saw it, whoever didn't rise to the top deserved to drown.

"Tell you what," Ocean said, tossing his ball to one of his friends. "Forget the Beausoleils—I'll trade you some water for those vegetables."

But Tanner knew Ocean all too well. He'd take the vegetables, then piss on Tanner's shoes and say, "There's your water."

"Thanks, but no thanks." Tanner pushed past him, while Ocean's friends snickered.

"Hey, Burgess," one of them shouted. "If you won't bathe, at least go home, put on a radiation suit, and spare us your stink!"

Tanner picked up the pace, trying to tune out their laughter.

Tanner found the front door unlocked and Mr. Beausoleil on the floor of his bedroom, moaning for help. He was dazed but not hurt. Tanner got the old man into a chair.

"Fell on my way to the bathroom," he told Tanner. "What's the point of legs when you can't use 'em anymore?"

"Where's Morena?"

"The marketplace," he said. "She found some things in the shed, thought she could sell. I told her she wouldn't get anything for the stuff, but she won't listen to me. Good God, what is that stench? Is that you, boy?"

Tanner put down his arms, clamping his pits closed. "Sorry."

"Grab yourself a jug of water! Sponge yourself down, for goodness' sake!"

"You barely have enough to drink," Tanner reminded him. "I'll survive a little bit of BO."

"Yes, but I may not!"

And then from behind him, Tanner heard, "He doesn't smell that bad."

He turned to see Morena. Like Tanner, she was fourteen. Like Tanner, she had lost her parents, and like Tanner, she was not a favorite of the clean-cuts.

"So did you sell anything?" the old man asked, and Morena shook her head. "It's my generation's fault." Mr. Beausoleil said. "When your parents were all children, we spent so much time teaching them about survival, we forgot to teach them compassion."

"I think it sucks the way they treat you," Tanner said. "You're the last of the original colonists—they ought to give you some respect."

Mr. Beausoleil considered it, looking down at his withered hands. "Things don't always turn out the way we expect," he said. "And I never expected to live this long."

"I'm glad you did, Grandpa." Morena brought a blanket and wrapped it around him. "Thanks for the food, Tanner. I'll cook us up some dinner."

After dinner, when the solar lights dimmed, they sat on the stainless steel porch and tried to imagine the new world, which was now less than a month away. But how can you imagine a world that curves downward when all you know is a world that curves up? How can you imagine sky when all you see when you look up is more ground? The teachers would show pictures of Earth in school, but only the most limited of images.

"You think they'd have given us more," Morena said. "More pictures, more music, more art."

"Maybe they wanted us to make our own art," Tanner suggested.

"Or maybe," offered Mr. Beausoleil, "they didn't think any of it mattered." There was a sadness in his voice. Some sort of regret that Tanner couldn't decipher.

"Why wouldn't it matter?" Tanner asked.

"Why, indeed."

The old man was silent for a long time, but Tanner knew he wasn't finished. Finally he said what was on his mind.

"Very few of the original builders came with us. Did you know that?"

"No," said Morena, moving a little closer. It also put her closer to Tanner. He thought he might put his arm around her but decided he'd better not.

"And the ones who did join the mission were all older than me—old enough to know they'd be dead before we reached Primordius. While the rest of us had families within a few years, none of the builders ever had children. I always found that strange."

Tanner could tell he was getting at something—perhaps something that had been bouncing around his mind for years but that he'd never spoke of. Until now.

"You know what else is strange," Mr. Beausoleil said. "The water shortage. You see, T-Bin is a closed system. Just about everything is recycled. We're like a bottle. Water doesn't escape from a closed bottle."

"Maybe there's a leak," Morena suggested.

"Yeah," agreed Tanner. "I know we've been hit by a few

meteors over the years. . . ."

The old man shook his head. "Dents and dings, nothing more." And then he brought his voice down to a whisper. "Computers are of little interest to most of the colonists now, but in my day, people knew how to use them—and I was pretty darn good at it too. Still am. So a few weeks ago, I did some checking. According to T-Bin's computers, there has been no water loss . . . but when you compare the volume of water being used now to when we were launched, there seems to be one-fifth less. That's millions of gallons. So the question is, where is it hiding?"

Suddenly something occurred to Tanner. "The Klingsmiths! I'll bet they're hoarding it! They're in charge of water distribution!"

Mr. Beausoleil pursed his lips and considered the suggestion. "Maybe," he said. "Or maybe it goes beyond that. Maybe the builders had more important plans for that water."

"What could possibly be more important than water for drinking and crop irrigation?" Tanner tried to wrap his mind around it, but like T-Bin's main road, it just came back to itself. As for Mr. Beausoleil, he leaned back in his chair and said nothing more.

* * *

A week later the entire population gathered in the town square for the unfurling ceremony. In the entire sixty-seven-year journey, there were only two such events. The first was at launch from Earth's orbit—when the massive solar sail was extended from the forward end of T-Bin and filled with the solar wind, which accelerated the ship to nearly a quarter the speed of light. Today it would deploy again, this time expanding behind them, catching the photons from their new sun and slowing them down like a solar parachute.

Tanner stood by Morena and Mr. Beausoleil, who was wobbly on his cane but insisted on standing for the event.

Governor Bainbridge stood on a platform in front of the huge statue dedicated to the builders. Stalwart figures looking forever skyward.

"Today we mark the final leg of our journey!" proclaimed Governor Bainbridge to the four hundred gathered. "As our bodies are merely vessels of the soul, so our great home is a vessel, delivering us, body and soul, to a glorious tomorrow on our shining new world."

"I may vomit," grumbled Mr. Beausoleil.

"Please, Grandpa," said Morena, "I'm trying to listen."

Tanner noted a few glowering glances from people around them. Some even moved away. It might have been

Tanner's odor that did it. He couldn't be sure.

"We were charged with the mission of spreading life to the stars," bellowed the governor. "Today we rededicate ourselves to that mission." He held out his hands, as if he wanted to hug everyone in the crowd. "You fine people are the precious cargo of this perilous journey. May you all be delivered to our new home in peace and safety—and when you finally look upon the first Primordial sunrise, you will know that nothing we've done has been in vain."

"He should bottle that speech and sell it as fertilizer," Mr. Beausoleil said loudly enough for everyone around them to hear. "Better than the chemical crap we use now."

Then a woman with a pinched face and hair pulled into a perfectly tight bun turned and said, "If you don't want to come, you can stay right here. I'm sure no one would mind." And although she said it to Morena's grandfather, Tanner couldn't help but notice that she made a point of glancing at all three of them.

The clock tower ticked down the seconds. Cheers erupted as the external cameras tracked the great sail deploying and stretching taut, filled with the solar wind. Now a new countdown began. Three weeks until T-Bin achieved orbit around Primordius. Ahead of them in the crowd, Tanner could see Ocean and his family hugging one another, filled with über-joy for their über-future. Tanner wanted to feel his own joyful anticipation—after all, once they left this tin can, he'd finally have the space to put some distance between himself and these people. Yet Tanner found himself filled instead with a prescient dread as wide and swollen as the great solar sail.

"From now until the day we arrive on the new world, our studies will be about preparing us for the transition."

Mrs. March, Tanner's teacher, wrote the word "colonists" on the board.

"We have called ourselves colonists all these years, but we won't truly be colonists until we arrive—and our new home will require us to give the very best of ourselves."

Tanner noticed that she held eye contact with him as she said it—as if warning him he'd better get with the program. Tanner glanced away and around the school room. With fewer than a hundred school-age children, kids of various ages were grouped together into four classrooms. The younger kids in his class looked terrified, the older kids confident. The goof-offs cracked jokes under their breath, and the studious kids actually took notes as if there would be a test after they disembarked.

"The planet will have *weather*." Mrs. March wrote the

word on the board. A lot of the kids looked confused, but no one admitted aloud that they had no idea what weather was. "Storms, and winds, and rain—which is beads of water falling from the sky. There may be extremes of heat and cold as well."

Something's wrong about this. The feeling pounded as powerfully as Tanner's heartbeat, but he couldn't figure out why he was so unsettled. It reminded him of when he used to play chess with his father. He would sense his loss three or four moves before it happened. He couldn't see all the moves that would lead him there—it was as if his brain saw something his conscious mind had yet to grasp. And everything about their arrival on Primordius screamed "checkmate."

"Fields will be rocky and hard to plant," continued Mrs. March, "and the only shelter will be shelter we find or build."

Then Ocean, slouching back in his chair, called out, "Will there be water enough for Tanner to take a bath?"

Snickers all around, and so Tanner said, "Will there be a cliff high enough for me to throw Ocean off?"

This time the only laugh came from Morena.

"Gentlemen, please," said Mrs. March. "Disparagement is not our friend." Then she paused and said. "But yes, there will be mountains, and yes, there will be water. A full half of the planet is water—not quite as much as Earth, but more than enough for us."

A younger child asked if there would be "things" in the water, and Mrs. March quieted his fears. "Primordius is a lifeless world, but its air is oxygen-rich, and ready for life. We are bringing that life—which is why Governor Bainbridge called us 'precious cargo.'" Then she smiled. "And all of you are the most precious of all—for you will be the first generation to grow up as Primordians."

That's the moment when one small piece of the puzzle presented itself to Tanner. He raised his hand, and Mrs. March took a deep breath before she called on him. "Yes, Tanner?"

"Why no animals?" he asked.

The question threw her off kilter. "Excuse me?"

"In Earth studies, we were always learning about animals. Pets and stuff that we don't eat, as well as animals that we do—but we didn't bring any. Why?"

"Ooh—I can answer that!" said Mary Wilcox, hurling her hand into the air so fast Tanner imagined her fingers flying off and embedding in the ceiling. "Animals eat too much, so if we brought them, we'd have to bring fewer people. So the builders decided we'd all be vegetarians, and there could be more of us on board."

"But if the mission is to spread life—" Tanner tried to point out, but Mrs. March cut him off.

"Mr. Burgess, I believe your question has been answered." Then she turned to the board and wrote the number 1.15. "Gravity on Primordius will be 1.15 times stronger than the centrifugal gravity we experience here. That might not seem like much, but it will make the physical demands on all of us very difficult."

Tanner's hand flew up again, and he spoke without waiting to be called on. "Then why didn't the builders slowly increase the spin of T-Bin, so we'd be accustomed to the new gravity by the time we got there?"

"The builders couldn't think of everything, Mr. Burgess."

"But they did!" called out Morena. "The builders planned out everything in T-Bin—it doesn't make sense they'd skip something so important."

"I'm sure they had their reasons," said Mrs. March. "Now please, we have a lot to cover in a limited amount of time. I will entertain no more questions today."

Day after day it was the same. Tanner would point out what appeared to be flaws in the builders' plans, only to be shut down by other students, or by Mrs. March.

"I think you're making some good points," Morena told him, "but maybe Mrs. March is right. The builders had their reasons. I mean, they only had two jobs. Build this place, and get us down to the planet safely. You'd think they'd get it right."

"Yeah, you'd think," Tanner told her. "And you'd also think that water wouldn't vanish into thin air."

With one week to Primordius, the entire school was taken on a field trip to an area of T-Bin that had been off limits for sixty-seven years. The "delivery ship" hangar. Within the massive hangar was a winged ship capable of carrying 400 people.

"The builders anticipated everything," explained Principal Hammond, who had taken charge of the tour. "Population growth was regulated to make sure there were precisely the same amount of colonists at the end of the journey as when the journey began. There's a seat for everyone."

"Where are the engines?" Tanner asked, and felt the communal groan of frustration from his classmates.

Principal Hammond, who was also seeing the delivery ship for the first time, looked it over, then said, "Well, clearly it's a glider."

"With no landing gear?" Morena asked, throwing a wink at Tanner.

"Obviously," said Principal Hammond, with increasing exasperation. "This craft was designed to land on water, which the autopilot will find. Believe me—nothing here has been left to chance. Nothing."

Two days and counting. Classes had ended. Anything they needed to learn either they already knew, or they would learn once they reached Primordius.

The T-Bin Council was in session nonstop, and a slow leak of rumors had people on edge. Rumors that T-Bin was not heading into geosynchronous orbit as expected. Rumors that the cargo bay of the delivery ship wasn't large enough to haul the farming equipment they would most certainly need. Rumors that the builders were not quite as visionary as everyone believed.

"So what?" Ocean Klingsmith was heard to say. "So we'll face a little hardship—it'll be good for us. And in the end, we'll conquer Primordius and live like kings. Or at least some of us will."

It was officially announced that there had been a slight miscalcuation, and T-Bin was not heading into any sort of orbit at all but was going to crash on Primordius instead.

"Not a problem," Governor Bainbridge told everyone. "We'll have left in the delivery ship long before it happens, and our departure is still on schedule."

On the last night, Morena showed up at Tanner's farm. Tanner had spent most of the day sorting and resorting the things he cared about into piles of things he *needed* to take with him versus the things that he *wanted* to take. He kept trying to whittle down his piles so that it would all fit into his backpack, but he simply couldn't do it. In the end, he realized, if he wanted to survive, he could take nothing but food and water. When Morena arrived it was a welcome relief, until he saw the tears in her eyes.

"You have to come!" Morena told him. "It's my grandfather! I called the doctor, but he wouldn't come! He wouldn't! He doesn't even care."

They ran all the way to the Beausoleil homestead to find Mr. Beausoleil looking so cadaverous in his bed, Tanner thought he might already be dead. But then he slowly opened his eyes.

"Glad," he wheezed. "Glad not to see it. Glad to die before we get there. Before it happens."

"Don't say that, Grandpa!" Morena took his hand. "You'll be on the ship with the rest of us. It's just one more day. You can hold on for one more day."

"Sorry . . ." he said. "So sorry for you, Morena. And for you, Tanner."

For a moment his rheumy eyes seemed to clear, and he held Tanner's gaze.

"You know something, don't you?" Tanner realized.

"Didn't know, but I suspected," the old man said. "So I did a little poking in the computer. There's a lot that's classified, but you can piece things together from the things that aren't classified." He grimaced. Shifted. He took a deep breath to ward off the pain, then closed his eyes, too weak to keep them open. "The storage silos," he said. "They're all sealed behind the aft wall of the T-Bin drum. Off limits. Computer controlled."

Tanner knew about the storage silos. They contained grains, chemical fertilizer, liquid oxygen—all the things that the colonists would need for a sixty-seven-year journey. No one had ever seen the storage area that held the silos, but everyone knew they were there. It was one more system that the builders had designed to work without any human interference.

"The silos should be empty. All used up," Mr. Beausoleil said. "*But every container is full.*"

Morena shook her head. "You must have misread it, Grandpa."

"But if it's true," Tanner said, "and we used up all the stuff in those silos . . . then what's in there now?"

Mr. Beausoleil's bony knuckles went white as he gripped Morena's hand tighter. "So, so sorry, Morena," he said, and then, before he released his final breath and let death take him, he hissed out one final prophecy.

"We are not the precious cargo. . . ."

Like the top and bottom of any tin can, there were two ends of the T-Bin drum. The colonists called the forward end "the lid," although it didn't open. Built into the steel face of the lid were the school, the medical center, the market, and various offices. At the other end of the drum was "the boot," and while the lid was designed to be aesthetically pleasing, with murals and mosaics layered into the steel, the boot was utilitarian and ugly. It held the physical plant that recycled water and reoxygenated the air when the plant life couldn't do it alone. It held the reactor that powered the lights and kept T-Bin from freezing in the icy depths of space—but the largest part of the boot was dedicated to the storage silos. Pipes went in, pipes went out, and the automated system worked so efficiently, there was no need for anyone to bother themselves with what was behind the great steel wall.

There was a hatch on that wall as intimidating as a vault

door that allowed entrance into the massive silo hold, but it had an angry red sign on it that read, Authorized Personnel Only. Apparently no one in T-Bin was authorized, for the door had never been opened.

On that last morning, with only a few hours left until the delivery ships launched, Morena and Tanner buried Mr. Beausoleil right in the heart of his farm. There were regulations against such things, but like always, no one cared enough about their comings and goings to stop them. Folks were too busy preparing for their future to worry themselves over the last rites of the only original colonist, or the troubles of two unclean orphans.

As soon as Tanner and Morena were done, and the requisite prayers had been said, they went straight to the silo hold.

The steel hatch had a security panel, and it required a password to be punched in. Tanner had never met a computer he couldn't hack—but this didn't even have an interface beyond the keypad. The only way to break in was to break the code.

While the rest of the colonists had a huge "Friendship Brunch," to gorge themselves on all the food they couldn't take with them, Tanner and Morena stood at the silo hold hatch and tried dozens upon dozens of passwords that failed.

Tanner kicked the door, which succeeded in doing nothing but bruise his toes. "I refuse to be defeated by a lousy password!"

"There's less than six hours until the delivery craft leaves, Tanner. Maybe we should forget this and start getting ready."

"No! Your grandfather was on to something." Tanner didn't care how limited the time was. That instinct that knew things three moves ahead was telling him that this was important. More than important, it was crucial.

"Look up there." He pointed to a brass plate above the door. It was a star chart that featured the area of space they were sailing into—or at least, how that area of space appeared from Earth. Seven stars in a pattern that had become familiar to everyone on T-Bin. "Where have you seen that before?"

"Everywhere," Morena said. "It's on the mural in our school, it's on the T-Bin flag—"

"No—I mean that exact brass plaque. I know I've seen it."

Morena squinted as she looked at it and said, "Town square. There's one just like it on the builders' monument."

"Bingo! Let's go."

They hurried to town square. In the center of the square

was the statue, and at its base was a lofty dedication carved in stone. Beside the dedication was the brass plaque of seven stars.

"I think you're right," Morena said. "There must be some connection."

Tanner stared at it, trying to put himself in the builders' places. Trying to think like them. Far away there was laughter from the Friendship Brunch, as if he was being mocked from a distance.

Morena did not have his patience. "Staring at that thing until your eyes cross isn't going to solve anything."

And then she gasped. When Tanner looked to her, her eyes looked odd somehow, and she was just a little bit pale.

"What is it?"

"Look at it again, Tanner—only this time cross your eyes!"

When he did, the stars were superimposed over the dedication, highlighting certain letters.

THIS MONUMENT IS *D*EDICATED TO THE VISION*A*RY DESIGNERS AND THE DA*R*ING SOULS *W*HO JOINED IN THIS GLORIOUS PARTNERSHIP TO BR*I*NG LIFE TO THE

STARS. THE I*N*TREPID AND THE BRAVE,
WE *C*OMMEND YOU!

What the stars spelled out was unmistakable.

DARWIN C.

Could it be that simple? Tanner and Morena rushed back to the silo hold door and, taking a deep breath, Tanner entered D-A-R-W-I-N-C.

Nothing at first. Then a clanging of bolts pulling back. The huge door began to open, and they were hit by a stink so overpowering it made them weak at the knees.

"Oh my God! What *is* that?" Morena covered her face and turned away.

The smell was so awful it took all of Tanner's will to step over the threshold. Inside, he saw the silo hold—row after row of steel tanks a hundred feet high. They were swollen to bursting—and all of them were oozing foul-smelling gunk. They were no longer full of grain, or whatever else they had once been carrying. One look at what oozed out of them and Tanner knew.

The silos were full of sewage.

A million flushes from sixty-seven years in space.

"I don't understand," said Morena, still covering her nose and mouth. "Waste water is recycled. And what can't be recycled is ejected into space."

"Apparently not."

This explained the missing water. Perhaps some of the water was recycled, but the rest was pumped right back into these vats of human waste.

"What were the builders *thinking*?" Morena wailed.

Tanner couldn't stand the stench for a moment more. He stumbled out with Morena, back into the fresh air of the T-Bin farmlands. As he caught his breath, it all fell into place, and he understood. He saw the minds of the builders, and he knew the truth. If your goal is to bring life to the stars, you don't start with the highest life-form. You start with the lowest.

"It was never the builders' plan to start a human colony!" Tanner told Morena. "Our sole purpose on T-Bin was to create sixty-seven years of bacteria. We are not the precious cargo. Our crap is!"

But before they could even process this woeful bit of news, T-Bin's spin-quake sirens began to blare—and this time it wasn't Tanner's doing.

There had only been one spin-quake in T-Bin's history. A meteor had clipped it and thrown the spinning drum several degrees off kilter. The force of the meteor strike had killed anyone in the wrong place at the wrong time, including Morena's parents. The hull wasn't breached, though, and ultimately the ball bearings that filled T-Bin's outer shell had done their job, flowing to where they needed to be, balancing the ship, and bringing its spin back under control.

However, this spin-quake was of a completely different nature. There was nothing in the ship's design to compensate for the gravitational pull of Primordius. T-Bin's smooth constant spin became a wobble growing more violent by the minute. It meant the timing of their departure was hours off—they were going to hit the planet much sooner than expected.

People left the Friendship Brunch in a panic, racing home to grab their belongings, if they lived close enough, or racing straight to the delivery craft hangar. The ground shifted beneath everyone's feet like a funhouse floor, the artificial gravity no longer pulling in a consistent direction.

On the main road, Tanner and Morena stopped people— trying to tell them what they knew, trying to warn them, but no one would listen. Finally they encountered Ocean Klingsmith.

"What the hell is wrong with the two of you?" he yelled. "Don't just stand there—get to the delivery ship."

For all of their rivalry, Tanner wasn't going to let Ocean run off blind. "The delivery ship isn't what you think it is, Ocean," Tanner said. "I don't think it's meant to save you—but I have an idea that might!"

"You're out of your mind!" Ocean said, and then he looked at Tanner in a way he never had before. Tanner actually saw compassion in his eyes. A seedling of humanity pushing its way through his arrogance. "Listen, Burgess— we haven't always been friends, but that doesn't matter now. We're all colonists. Come with me, both of you. Get on the delivery ship, and if you want to argue, we can argue after we land."

Tanner shook his head. "I won't set foot on that ship, Ocean—and neither should you!"

Any compassion in Ocean's eyes vanished as quickly as it had come. "Fine—stay here and die here for all I care. It's what you deserve."

Then he ran off to join the others.

Morena turned to Tanner. "If you really do have a plan, you had better tell me about it."

Tanner sighed. "I will. But you're not gonna like it."

The delivery ship launched from T-Bin. All colonists were accounted for except for two. With just a few minutes left until T-Bin entered the planet's atmosphere, Tanner and Morena raced from Tanner's homestead toward the silo hold, both of them wearing radiation suits. Around them, entire orchards were uprooted by the spin-quake. Patches of earth flew past them as if they had been ripped up by a tornado. It was almost impossible to keep a sure footing as gravity kept shifting beneath them.

"This is pointless!" Morena yelled as they ran. "Nothing can save us—T-Bin is going to crash and burn."

"It's going to crash," Tanner agreed. "But it's not going to burn. If it burns, then the mission fails."

"But the radioactive core —"

"If I'm right about this, it will be ejected into space. The builders wouldn't risk contaminating the planet with radiation."

And sure enough, as they approached the silo hold hatch, all of T-Bin was plunged into darkness. It could only mean that the core had just ejected.

They stumbled over tree roots and bits of the buckling road in the dark until they came into the silo hold. Here, emergency lights every ten yards gave them enough light to see the curves of the silos but nothing more. The stench was unbearable, and Tanner could hear the sloshing of the awful stuff within the silos. As bad as it smelled now, he knew it was going to get a whole lot worse. He sealed the soft helmet of his radiation suit, activated its oxygen supply, and found the ladder on silo #106.

"Start climbing," he told Morena.

She glared at him through the face mask of her radiation suit. "Do we really have to do this?"

"Do you have a better idea?"

She didn't answer him. Instead, she started climbing. "I hate you for this."

But that was all right. She wouldn't hate him for long if they survived. And she wouldn't hate him for long if they died, either.

When they reached the top, Tanner opened the silo hatch and peered inside. Darkness—but he knew what was in there. Rather than thinking, he just jumped, submerging himself in the sickening stew. The stuff was thicker than mud. Maybe—just maybe—it was thick enough to absorb the force of a crash landing. In a moment he felt Morena beside him, and he grabbed onto her. Now there was nothing to do but wait, and listen to the metallic groaning of the ship around them as it fell from space and into the atmosphere of Primordius.

Ocean Klingsmith, like most of the T-Bin colonists, trusted the designers' master plan. Even after T-Bin failed to settle into geosynchronous orbit. Even after the spin-quake forced everyone to evacuate earlier than planned, he still trusted the designers to deliver them to the new world safely.

As the delivery ship hit the atmosphere, it shuddered violently. Ocean could feel his teeth rattle, so he clenched his jaw. The air in the cabin grew warm, but the shields protecting the craft from the searing heat of reentry did their job. The ship held together. Finally, through the small oval windows of the craft, clouds came into view, white and puffy, just like images they had seen of Earth. The air became turbulent as they hit the clouds.

"Normal!" called out Governor Bainbridge, who sat in the front row. "Not to worry, turbulence is normal."

Even so, Ocean gripped onto the harness that held him in his seat. The computer flying their huge glider banked them to the left. *Toward water,* he thought—*maybe even the kind of water I'm named for.* He could imagine the craft landing smoothly on an ocean and coming to rest where the waters kissed the shore. They would step out, like the pilgrims on Plymouth Rock, and claim this world as their own.

But it didn't happen that way.

When the delivery ship punched through the clouds, the colonists weren't met with an ocean vista. Instead they were met with the prospect of a jagged mountain range. Those looking out of the windows gasped in fear.

"It's all right," Governor Bainbridge said. "The ship knows what it's doing. It can navigate us out of this."

They flew between the jagged peaks, banking left and right—then suddenly the entire dome of the delivery ship ripped away, exposing them to the sky. They were pummelled by a violent force none of them had ever felt before.

Wind! thought Ocean, in a panic. *This is wind!* He could barely keep his eyes open against it, but he forced himself to look, and what he saw explained everything. Up ahead, the front row of seats were jettisoned skyward, sending Bainbridge and a dozen others up and out.

Of course! Ocean thought. *These are ejection seats!* It made perfect sense; the delivery ship was doing exactly what it was supposed to do! It couldn't find a safe place to land, so it was ejecting everyone to safety, sending them down by parachute. Ingenious! The designers thought of everything!

The second row ejected. Then the third. Finally, it was Ocean's turn. He gripped the harness, closed his eyes, and felt the sudden surge of force as he, and everyone beside him, was shot out into the open air of Primordius.

He opened his eyes, waiting for the parachute to open.

He was still shooting forward at an incredible speed—he hadn't even begun to fall yet. Up ahead he saw the stone face of a cliff. *The parachute will open any second now . . . ,* Ocean thought. *Any second . . .*

But it didn't. And it finally dawned on him that maybe there were no parachutes. For anyone.

No! This can't be! Ocean's mind screamed as the face of the cliff swelled before him. *I'm a clean-cut! I'm the best and the brightest! I'm the future of humanity! I'm . . . I'm . . .*

Ocean Klingsmith hit the face of the cliff at 200 miles per hour—so fast that his body liquefied like a bug on a windshield. The chair fell away, leaving a big red splat on the mountain—proof positive that the delivery ship did exactly what it was designed to do: deliver its payload of warm, nutrient-rich biological material to Primordius.

The massive drum of the Transtellar Bacterial Injector—T-Bin for short—burst through the atmosphere, delivering a sonic boom to announce the arrival of life on Primordius. It plunged through the upper atmosphere, showing no sign of slowing down.

Within silo #106, Tanner and Morena clung to each other, afraid to be alone within the foulness around them. The fall through the atmosphere, the not knowing where or how this would end, was beyond terrifying. With their face masks pressed close, they couldn't see through the muck, but they could hear each other's muffled voices as they tried to comfort one another, until the roar of reentry drowned out everything.

Outside, the great drum, still smoking from reentry, plummeted in freefall, but the icy air of the upper atmosphere cooled it. Then, once it hit the dense, cloud-spotted air of the lower atmosphere, a multilayered array of massive parachutes deployed, slowing its descent.

Within silo #106, the sudden pull of the opening parachutes sent Tanner and Morena plunging deeper in the thick brown miasma but not quite to the bottom. All was silent then.

"Are we dead?" Tanner heard Morena say. "I think we're dead."

"Not yet," Tanner told her. But he knew that one way or another, it would all be over soon.

Even with a mile-wide array of parachutes to slow it down, T-Bin was far too heavy for a gentle landing. As it swooped into a valley where the mountainsides were curiously speckled with hundreds of red measle-like spots, it struck a jutting peak, then another, then another, until finally it began to rupture.

When T-Bin struck the first peak, Tanner and Morena were hurled sideways within their silo of sewage, but Tanner had been right—the stuff was so thick that it absorbed the worst of it. It acted like a gelatinous shock absorber. They struck the side of the silo but not hard enough to do anything more than shake them up.

The second and third strikes were worse. They bounced back and forth, and they could hear the crunch of tearing metal. "This is it," Tanner shouted in the darkness, gripping Morena tighter.

Then, five seconds later, their world ended.

When the great interstellar drum hit the valley floor, it tore completely apart, spreading its inner lining of farmland in a deluge of soil, shredded plants, and splintered trees that rained upon the valley.

The bacteria-rich storage silos broke free, the swollen canisters bursting as they hit the landscape, spewing fetid filth upon the jagged rocks from one end of the valley to the other.

Silo #106 tumbled end over end, until it finally split open, spilling forth its bubbling nastiness, along with two kids, who came to rest in a shallow pond of the viscous sludge.

The two had been pulled apart by the force of the

deluge, and Tanner frantically searched for Morena, trying to wipe the grunge from his facemask but succeeding only in spreading it like finger paint. For one panicked moment, he thought that she had been thrown out of range, or worse, impaled upon the jagged metal of the burst silo. He ripped off his helmet, ignoring the gut-wrenching smell around him, and he saw her struggling to stand on shaky legs. She fell over into the stuff, clearly too dizzy to stand, and just gave up. She sat in it, waist deep, until Tanner arrived, helped her up, and they climbed onto the first boulder they could find that wasn't covered with yuck.

He helped her take off her radiation helmet and smiled at her. "Welcome to Primordius!" he said, and Morena smiled back.

"Crash," she said, "but no burn."

"Told ya!"

Finally they took in their surroundings. They were in a great valley between towering peaks. There was a massive scar miles long where T-Bin had crashed. Now the great steel drum lay in two jagged halves, like a broken egg, and its innards lay strewn across the entire valley. They also saw the wreck of the delivery ship. There were no signs of survivors. Not even bodies. Tanner didn't want to consider why that might be. Then, as he looked out over a pungent valley of funk, something occurred to him.

"You know what this is? This is primordial soup! The bacteria will grow. It will get carried by the wind. It will evolve!"

"And what about us?"

Tanner considered the question. "The seeds from T-Bin are all over this valley. This stuff around us might be nasty, but it's fertilizer. Plants will grow, and in a single season, there'll be stuff to eat—and in the meantime, there's plenty of food packed in the cargo hold of the delivery ship."

Morena nodded. "It would never have been enough to feed an entire colony," she said, "but it'll be enough to feed the two of us."

"And," added Tanner, "we can use the parachutes to build ourselves shelter. . . . To build us a home."

Tanner and Morena took a long look at each other, both stunned by the implications of all this. The two of them. Alone. In the single life-filled valley on an otherwise dead planet. A valley that would soon be a garden.

"Let's move upwind before I hurl," Morena finally said.

"Sounds like a plan."

About a mile upwind, where the stench of new life faded, they found a fresh spring forming a small lake. The water hadn't been fouled by "Brown Betty," which was the name they'd already given the pungent stew of microorganisms that now flavored the rest of the valley.

By the side of the lake, they shed their dirty radiation suits. Tanner found that his own personal fragrance now smelled fresh and sweet compared with the malodor of Brown Betty. The air around them was crisp—cooler than what they were used to in T-Bin but not so cold as to be uncomfortable. It was refreshing—and the water of the spring was steaming and warm to the touch.

"I've been thinking," Morena said as they gazed at the rising steam of the crystal-clear water. "The builders never truly intended to start a colony, except for a bacterial colony, right?"

"Yeah. . . ."

"And yet they provided that riddle—the star code that let us break into the silo hold. That means that they *wanted* someone to figure it all out, Tanner. Maybe not the whole colony, but someone smart enough—clever enough—to uncover the truth and come up with a way to survive."

Tanner realized she was right. The clean-cuts were always talking about survival of the fittest, and how it was the builders' driving philosophy—but the builders had a very different idea of what that meant. It made him feel noble to know he was the kind of survivor they had in mind.

"I don't know about you," Tanner said, "but I could use a bath."

Morena smiled. "You read my mind."

They stripped down to their skivvies, which might have felt awkward before today, but after what they had been through, nothing felt awkward anymore.

Together they dove into the warm spring water, and for the first time in as long as he could remember, Tanner Burgess felt sparkling clean.

PLAN B

BY REBECCA STEAD

Wednesday
April 19

Dear _____ ,

Because whoever is reading this, I have no idea who you
are. I haven't even figured out where I'm going to stick this
thing when I'm done with it, but it'll be somewhere secret,
somewhere hard to find, and it might be a long time before
anyone reads it. A year. Ten years. Maybe more.

You can't write a text or an email and hide it for someone to find someday. You need pen and paper for that. And
opposable thumbs. Speaking of which: I probably should
have started this letter hours ago, when I heard the key

turn on the other side of my bedroom door.

I keep listening for the sound of the lock and squinting to see if maybe the doorknob is turning. But I don't know if I'm hoping that the door will burst open or stay closed. I don't even know how much longer I'm going to be able to hold this pen.

Opposable thumbs. Let me tell you something, whoever-you-are: If you have opposable thumbs, you probably take them for granted. If you knew how much you love your thumbs, you would write them a love song, sing it in your underwear, and post it on YouTube. You would be willing to totally humiliate yourself for those thumbs.

And if you don't have opposable thumbs? Well, that would answer a lot of the questions I have running through my head right now.

Let's just say I hope you have thumbs.

I wasn't supposed to tell anyone about us. Obviously. But when sixth grade started last year, I finally found a real friend. And I had kept this big secret inside me for such a long time.

Mom says I've got "forty-nine good friends," and yeah, we have the monthly Skypes with the others: Caleb from California, Isaac from Indiana, Toby from Texas, Cody from Colorado, and so on. But the Skypes are so awkward, with all the parents looking nervous in the background. A big part of friendship is just hanging out with nobody watching. Which is hard to do when you know all the grown-ups are scrutinizing (vocab word!) everyone else's skin.

Evan is different. He moved to New York City last year, and he's just a good friend, you know? He laughs at everything, even when the joke is on him. And he's not worried all the time, like me. And one day this winter I just—said it. I told him about us. All I wanted was for someone to know me, to understand me. I hate hiding. And, like, pretending all the time. I've been pretending my whole life, pretty much.

I knew Evan wouldn't flip out on me, and he didn't. He was real cool about it, all things considered. And I'm so much happier, having someone I can talk to about real stuff. But right now I'm worried about him. He was supposed to come over after school today, after my appointment with the doctors. What if he stops by with a bag of Ms. Pena's empanadas?

Did I mention I'm missing Foods of Spain Day?

Yeah. While I'm locked in here, Señora Pena is bringing all this amazing food to school to share with our Spanish class.

I mention Foods of Spain Day because I'm kind of hungry. Everyone totally freaked out this morning, and the question of lunch never really came—

Man! I just fell asleep. Second time that's happened since I got locked in here! Maybe the third time.

I haven't heard anything through the door in a while.

I wonder if my parents are okay.

I wonder what the doctors are doing right now.

And if Evan shows up with those empanadas, what will they do to him?

Maybe the empanadas are just wishful thinking.

I'm going to tell you what happened now. (Sorry, Mr. Barker, I know that was a terrible transition. I should have said something like, "speaking of thumbs, here's what happened," or even better: "speaking of being locked in my room, here's what happened." So I hope you aren't a sixth-grade English teacher, because if you are, this letter will probably annoy—

Shoot, I think I just fell asleep again.

So here's what happened:

Five days ago, when we got back from our vacation in

Florida, Mom said to dump all our stuff on the floor right inside the front door. She was carrying the beach bag, with the sandy plastic buckets and shovels, the Kadima paddles, and the fake sunscreen, and she let the whole thing just drop off her shoulder and spill out all over the floor, which was weird because Mom always pretends to be this perfect person with a perfect husband, a perfect son (that's me), and a perfect house. (Or in our case, a perfect apartment.) I watched the little rubber Kadima ball bounce a couple of times and then roll under the hall table, where my school-books were neatly stacked, ready for school on Monday. She didn't even notice. I figured she was still thinking about the fish fry that we never made it to.

When we checked into the hotel in Florida, they told us about the Saturday Night Fish Fry Extravaganza, and how it was free for guests who stay the full week. A big dinner with lots of families is just the kind of thing Mom loves more than anything. It proves she's doing everything right. I knew she was thinking that the other mothers hadn't even thought twice about our family: That we were—that Mom had *made* us—that good. And me most of all. I was perfect. Undetectable.

But apparently not perfect enough.

Because when Mom saw what was happening to me on

Saturday morning, we had to rush off even before breakfast. We didn't say goodbye to any of the other families, except for the one in the next-door cabin, and that was only because they saw us packing up our rental car in a hurry and asked if everything was okay.

Mom told them I had a broken arm. Which made them look at us kind of funny because I was carrying two bags to the car at that very moment. When Mom is flustered she sometimes messes up. She really is very good at what she does, most of the time.

The cats came running as soon as we opened the apartment door, except Toto, who always likes to play it cool, like, "Oh, were you guys gone? I'm so darn busy and independent, I didn't even notice."

Dad bent down and shook hands with the cats. Alex first, then Aidan.

"Steven!" Mom yelled. "You have got to stop shaking hands with the cats!"

Dad and I stared at each other for a second. Mom isn't usually a yeller.

"Want to go through the mail?" Dad asked her, holding out a thick pile of catalogs and envelopes. He was trying to cheer her up. Mom loves mail. Dad says that on the Boat, "mail box" was her favorite game.

But Mom shook her head at him. "Shower," she said. "Now."

Like all the parents, Mom showers twice a day, every day. Even that day.

Alex and Aidan, who are only half-grown, started playing with the Kadima ball, batting it down the hall and then running after it like it was a live thing trying to escape them.

"Check the cats' water dish, Nathan," Dad said, not looking at me. "Please." I knew he was struggling to be nice, because what happened in Florida wasn't my fault. It wasn't my fault at all.

The kitchen was a mess of eggshells and open tuna cans. There was a dirty frying pan on a hot plate on the floor. "And who's supposed to clean *this* up?" I said out loud to myself while I stood at the sink and waited for the cats' water dish to fill up. "Me, I'm guessing?"

Toto padded up behind me and rubbed against my ankle. Since he doesn't show a lot of affection, I figured he was saying sorry for the mess. Still, sometimes I wished Dad had never taught the cats to cook in the first place.

I put the water dish on the kitchen floor and sat next to

it, letting Toto walk across my lap and then lie down on my legs. Toto's real name is Bartolomej. Mom says I started calling him "Toto" when I was practically still a baby, because I couldn't even come close to saying "Bartolomej."

A few minutes later Mom came in wearing the sundress I knew she'd been saving for the fish fry.

"Sigh," she said.

Uh-oh.

Mom only said "sigh" when she was at rock bottom.

She started saying it when she was just a kid on the Boat, because she had misunderstood the teacher. She didn't get that a sigh was a thing you DID, not a thing you SAID. So whenever she wanted to express 1) frustration, 2) deep sadness, 3) transcendent happiness, or 4) sarcasm, she said "sigh."

Mom is a top-of-the-class sort of person, always studying and practicing, so by the time someone noticed she was mixed up and corrected her, it was hard for her to erase the habit. She did, though. Of course she did.

So now when she's 1) frustrated, which is sometimes; 2) deeply sad, which is not so much, luckily; 3) transcendently happy, which doesn't happen so much either as far as I can tell; or 4) sarcastic, which she never is, Mom sighs just like everyone else.

Except every once in a while, when she's really upset, she slips and says "sigh" instead. When that happens, Dad and I usually start telling her that her skin looks great and volunteering to help with stuff.

"I'll clean all this up," I said quickly, waving toward the open tuna cans, the upside-down egg cartons, and the cats' omelet pan. "How was your shower? Your skin looks good, Mom. Wow. Skin looks great."

"Oh." She glanced at her shoulder, then held out one arm and sort of flipped it back and forth. "Yeah. Thanks, honey."

I looked at my watch. "I guess they're firing up the fish fry about now, huh?"

Dumb. Why had I said that? Sometimes when something is on my mind, it comes out of my mouth by accident.

Mom slid down next to me on the floor. "Oh, honey. Who cares about a fish fry? I mean, there are more important things than a stupid hotel party. You know?"

I guess I don't always know what Mom is thinking after all. (And she said "stupid"!)

She started petting Toto, who pretended not to notice, and we just sat there until Toto finally gave up his pride and started purring. And after a little while Mom took a deep breath, opened her mouth, and said, "sigh."

* * *

We were still sitting like that on the floor when Dad came in and said, "I spoke to the doctors. We have an appointment for Wednesday."

"Wednesday?" Mom said. "But I thought they'd want to see him right away."

Dad shook his head. "The Boat is on the far side."

"They're bringing the Boat? Is that really necessary?" Mom looked at me. "You look sleepy. Are you sleepy? You should go to bed."

Mom stood next to me while I brushed my teeth, first with regular toothpaste, then with the special kind they send us every month from the Boat. She stared at my reflection in the mirror the whole time, like she thought it might start talking to her.

I didn't realize until I was getting into bed that it was only about 5 p.m. But I actually was super tired, so I didn't bother to argue. In fact, I think I slept on and off through the whole next day and didn't really wake up until Monday.

Monday morning, I opened my eyes to find Toto standing on my chest, just looking at me.

"I'm guessing Mom forgot to feed you?" I said. I picked out a T-shirt and a pair of extra-baggy shorts and we wandered toward the kitchen.

No sandy buckets by the front door, no hot plate on the kitchen floor. The apartment smelled like toast. I shook a bunch of food into the cats' dish and then sat down to eat breakfast. All the usual cereal boxes were on the table. Mom came out of her room and watched me pour a little from each box into my bowl, but I couldn't seem to eat much. Not with her staring at me like that.

She reached across the table and felt my forehead.

I shook her off. "What's going to happen at the appointment on Wednesday?" I asked.

She must not have heard me, though. She just stood up and touched the skin on her face.

"Skin looks great, Mom."

She smiled. "Thanks, honey."

I suddenly felt like I might explode. Not literally. But I couldn't wait to get to school. To Evan.

I still don't know who you are (obviously) but you know what? I'm already feeling a little better. Like you and I are friends or something, which is weird, because I know I'm still alone in here. It's hard to explain. It's just, like, better.

*　*　*

Mr. Barker, my English teacher, would hate that "like" up there. He'd circle it and put a bunch of exclamation points next to it, like—!!!!!!

But this letter is for you, not for Mr. Barker, and I want you to know the real me before it's too late. And if you *are* Mr. Barker, um, sorry about that. Please don't, like, flunk me.

Actually, it probably doesn't matter if you do.

Mom loves that I say "like," just like all the real Americans. I sound like a native. And that was the plan. Everything was going great, until last Saturday morning in Florida.

Most people don't really know how big the Earth is, compared to its moon.

In case you're one of them, it's easy:

Pretend you have a big ball of Play-Doh.

Now, in your head, divide that big ball into fifty small Play-Doh balls, all the same size.

Pick up one of those fifty balls, and set it aside.

Now take the other forty-nine balls and smush them back together into one big ball.

Hold the big ball in one hand and the small ball in the other. That's pretty much the Earth and the moon.

*   *   *

Now take the moon ball and divide it into a ten million smaller balls. Pick up one of those and you're holding the Mothership. Also known as the Boat. That's where my parents grew up, mostly, on the way to your planet.

What happened in Florida is something we never even worried about. It's dawning on me that right behind all the things I *actively* worry about is a whole *universe* of things I didn't even know I should be worrying about. And once you know there's a universe of stuff you don't know, you begin to wonder how big it is and how many bad things are in it.

Warning: bad transition number two.

Here's the thing that happened last Saturday in Florida:

Early in the morning, I reached for my blue swimsuit. I swam in the pool every morning with Dad, who is still trying to get over his natural-born hatred of water. Mom also got me an orange one with sharks on it, but it's a little young for a twelve-year-old.

What happened was I couldn't get the swimsuit on. I know that sounds weird. I mean, I stepped into it, one leg, then the other, but I couldn't pull it up all the way. It just wouldn't go. So, okay, I figured maybe Mom had accidentally shrunk it in one of the power dryers in the laundry room down the pebble path from our cabin. She liked to hang out there and chat with the other moms. She said it kept her skills sharp.

I tried the orange suit with the sharks on it, but it wouldn't pull up all the way either. It was like there was something sticking out of my, um, lower back—I felt around a little. And started shouting.

When she rushed in and saw why I was yelling, Mom pretty much turned white. That's what happens when she stops regulating her blood—it all falls straight down to her feet. She gets pale and has about a minute to get it moving again before she faints. Because I'm a first-gen, I've been regulating since I was born, and I don't even have to think about it, but Mom lived a long time before she ever came here, and sometimes when she's startled (or horrified, I guess) she forgets.

Anyway, Dad walked in, took one look at her, and barked "Rachel! Blood!" And Mom nodded and her color came back.

"What is it?" I said, twisting around and trying to see whatever it was on my back. "Am I dying?"

"No! Of course not," Dad said. "It's just . . . well. . ." He looked at Mom. "It's your tail, son. Your tail is growing back."

*　*　*

At school on Monday, Evan was really nice about it. "Dude, my tonsils grew back, did I ever tell you that? I had them out when I was five, and three years later—*Boom!* They're back, and I'm snoring like a trucker again."

I looked at him. "Did they grow out of your *butt*?" This was after two cups of coffee. Lately I have to drink coffee in the morning or I fall asleep in school.

"I was a total mouth-breather," Evan said, shaking his head. "I had to get them cut out all over again."

Which I really did not want to think about.

One doctor was tall and one was short, and when they showed up today (a.k.a. Wednesday, a.k.a. Foods of Spain Day) they were both fresh from their morning showers—I could smell the special soap on them. I thought they might be mad at me, because tails were definitely not part of the plan. They had not spent twelve years crossing the galaxy, training my parents and all the others, and figuring out how to make themselves look less like cats and more like humans just to have me ruin everything by growing my tail back.

But they didn't seem mad at all. In fact, they were smiling. They asked to see my tail. Then for a long time they measured and looked and pointed out things to each other

171

that I hadn't even noticed, about the slight angle my eyes were taking toward the back, and that I had some orange fuzz on my arms and legs.

"It's working," the tall one said finally. "It's working!"

"We can stay!" the short one said. And they hugged, which was weird, because cats, even cats that look like humans, are not naturally huggy.

Mom looked confused. Dad cleared his throat and said he didn't see how my tail could be good news.

One of the doctors clomped him on the back. "This means that we can do it, we can transform the human race. Earth will be ours!"

"But—*we're* trying to become *human!*" Mom burst out. "Not the other way around!"

They nodded. "Oh, yes," the tall one said. "We tried that. And it might have been all right. Only it didn't work." He looked Mom and Dad over. "You two still look pretty good. Excellent, even. But some of the others are in bad shape. They're looking distinctly—feline. We've had to take them back on board."

"Back on the Boat?" Mom gasped. Her gasp is excellent. "Who?"

The short one ticked them off on his fingers: "New

Mexico, Georgia, Utah . . ."

"Trust me," the tall one said, "this is going to be much better. All cats, just like at home. The humans will probably enjoy being cats!"

I felt for my tail and found it considerably longer than when I'd checked that morning.

"This is crazy!" Mom said. "Nathan is one of *us*. How does his tail prove anything?"

"That's right," Dad said. "He's simply reverting to his natural state. Maybe he just needs to take more showers."

Both of the doctors broke into big smiles. "What you don't know," the tall one said, "is that Nathan *is* a human. All of the children are human!"

The short one nodded. "Little human laboratories, incubating different strains of the virus for us."

"Virus?" Dad said.

Mom reached out and pulled me to her.

"Oh, yes. We've created many different strains over the years. But none of them has worked. Until now."

"But—when did you give it to him? How?" Mom was squeezing me really hard.

"It was in the toothpaste. But I think when it comes to the general population, infecting the water supply will be much more efficient. We'll take little Nathan here back to the Boat, do a full exam, and watch him complete his transformation. And when—"

"Nathan has school!" Mom interrupted.

The doctors stared at her. "School! Don't you understand? That's all irrelevant now! He can't stay here, obviously. We need to confirm our results with some of the other children, and then all that remains is the dissemination of the virus. It's perfect, really—New York City is a great place to start. Eight million people!"

I don't know exactly when during this conversation Mom forgot to keep her blood moving, but this is when she fainted. And then Dad freaked and started throwing punches.

But with Mom out cold on the floor, it was two against one. I tried to help, but the doctors wrestled Dad into a chair and tied him to it. And then they locked me in my room. To wait for the Boat.

They must have woken Mom up, because right after that I heard her voice through my bedroom door. She sounded a little crazy, shouting "Toto, Plan B! Toto, Plan B!"

Toto, in case you don't remember, is OUR CAT. It must have been the oxygen deprivation.

It's funny to think of Evan, and how much I wanted to be like him. And it turns out that we're more alike than I thought. We were both adopted, for one thing. Except I was more, like, stolen.

I think someone is trying to open the door.

Debriefing of Undercover Agent Bartolomej after termination of "Operation Earth."

Supervisor: What the heck happened here yesterday? You're supposed to be one of our top guys.

Agent B: You have my report.

Supervisor: There are a few holes.

Agent B: It was complicated. Have an empanada.

Supervisor: It's always complicated, Agent B.

Agent B: This was different.

Supervisor: I'm listening.

Agent B: It's Agent R. She was . . a challenge.

Supervisor: No kidding. That's what you were supposed to be here for. To notice if anyone was slipping. To report it.

Agent B: She wasn't slipping. She never slipped.

Supervisor: What are you telling me?

Agent B: She was perfect. But there was something going on that I couldn't see.

Supervisor: Because you weren't looking hard enough.

Agent B: Because it was impossible to detect.

Supervisor: What was it?

Agent B: It was love.

Supervisor: Love?

Agent B: Agent R loved the boy. Her boy.

Supervisor: The kid was human, Agent. He was a means to an end.

Agent B: Are you going to try an empanada or not?

Supervisor: Maybe just one. But I still don't understand what you're trying to tell me about Agent R.

Agent B: I'm telling you that she was Nathan's mother.

Supervisor: And?

Agent B: And she cared about him more than she cared about the mission.

Supervisor: Nobody cared about the mission more than Agent R. This is delicious. What did you say it's called?

Agent B: It's an empanada. Maybe Agent R wasn't exactly who you thought she was.

Supervisor: Yeah, I figured that out when she commandeered the Boat and took off with Agent S and the kid. And every ounce of the virus.

Agent B: Indeed.

Supervisor: The doctors reported that at one point Agent R shouted something about a "Plan B." Did you hear that? It wasn't in your report.

Agent B: I don't recall that.

Supervisor: You don't recall that? It's the last thing the doctors remember before they woke up in an empty apartment. Empty except for your team, I mean.

Agent B: Keep in mind that the doctors had just been assaulted by Steven—excuse me, by Agent S. They may have been temporarily confused. It's all in my report.

Supervisor (consulting file): And apparently she called out the name "Toto." Were you aware of anyone on the premises she might have referred to as Toto?

Agent B: Of course not. It would have been in my report.

Supervisor: There's something else: How do you think Agent R learned to navigate the Boat? She was only a kid on the trip to Earth.

Agent B: She must have been watching.

Supervisor: You should know. It was your job to watch her.

Agent B: (no response)

Supervisor: You're a trained engineer, Agent B, isn't that right?

Agent B: (no response)

Supervisor: Did you teach Agent R how to drive the Boat?

Agent B: We had a lot of time on our hands.

Supervisor: You realize that without the Boat we're all stranded here? You do understand that, Agent B?

Supervisor: (no response)

Supervisor: I hope you have plans. Our resources are limited. You can't expect us to take you in after what's happened.

Agent B: Don't worry about me. I'll be fine.

Supervisor: Where will you go?

Agent B: I have something lined up.

Supervisor: Where did these empanadas come from?

Agent B: A friend stopped by earlier.

Supervisor: How the heck do you have friends? You're deep undercover as a house pet.

Agent B: Are we done? I have to pack.

Supervisor: One last thing: No one can figure out how Agent R boarded the Boat without a key. It should have been impossible.

Agent B: It certainly is a puzzle.

Supervisor: My records indicate that you have a set of keys to the Boat. They aren't much use now, but I've been told to collect them.

Agent B: (no response)

Supervisor: Can you produce those keys, Agent?

Agent B: I seem to have misplaced them.

Supervisor: You're stating that you have misplaced the keys?

Agent B: Alex and Aidan played with them on occasion. You remember—my trainees.

Supervisor: Played with them?

Agent B: Training exercises.

Supervisor: Agent B, we are on the record here. Can you or can you not locate your keys to the Mothership?

Agent B: I cannot tell you the precise location of my keys. End of story.

Supervisor: End of story?

Agent B: End of story.

A Day in the Life

BY SHAUN TAN

wake to the sound of
a solitary cicada.

stumble across my own consciousness
in the kitchen - what time is it?

still night, according to
the snow dome: back to bed!

Some hours later, wait out
front for the coffee machine.

(glad I remembered to pay my rates)

let the iguanas out the back.

answer some emails from
three years ago.

begin work on the most
profound story ever conceived.

later realise it's all utter nonsense.

deliver a monologue on artistic failure
in the office of my inner budgie.

eventually realise
a simple truth.

let the iguanas back in
and think about tomorrow.

THE KLACK BROS. MUSEUM
BY KENNETH OPPEL

When the train arrives in Meadows, it seems to Luke to be just like all the other forlorn places they've stopped along the way.

Over the PA system a woman says, "Ladies and gentlemen, our station stop will be longer than scheduled. A freight train has derailed up the track. We'll be here roughly five hours."

Five hours. What's five more hours in an already endless trip?

"Want some fresh air?" his father asks.

Luke looks out the window. There is a gravel parking lot

beside the weather-beaten station. Curling shingles, water dripping from a busted downspout. Across the road are several bleak houses whose front windows look onto the tracks. In one window he spots an elderly couple sitting side by side on lawn chairs, peering out. The man raises a pair of binoculars to his eyes.

"See that?" Luke says to his Dad. "This is big excitement in Meadows."

They step off the train. The air has a bite to it. There is snow on the rooftops, and on the grass. Luke looks back at the train, the rolling torture chamber that's been taking them across the country. He's spent two nights aboard it already. It is March break and Dad has decided this would be a good trip for them to take together. Mom's with Olivia in Fort Lauderdale. Luke wishes he were on the beach in Florida, looking at palm trees. There would be girls to look at too. As it is, he is the youngest person on the train— not counting the crying baby that belongs to the exhausted couple from England. Even his Dad is young compared with most of the passengers.

"I didn't want to come on this trip."

"You're loving this trip," his father says distractedly.

"If you say so."

His father sighs and looks at him. "Not at all?"

Luke shrugs. Shrugging is very efficient. It could mean anything. Mom says it's rude.

"So what's your idea of a good time?" Dad wants to know.

"Just staying at home, chilling, hanging out with my friends."

"You can do that anytime."

Another shrug. "It kinda sucks. There's nothing to do."

"I've told you, it's a trip I've wanted to take for a long time."

"Cause you're blocked."

He sees his father inhale and frown. His father's a writer and hates that word. "Possibly."

"I don't see why I had to get dragged along."

"Well, you can't always get what you want," his father says, and then starts singing the Rolling Stones song. Luke hates it when his father does this. Whenever his father thinks Luke's complaining too much, he starts singing, looking very soulful and intense, and snapping his fingers in time.

"Please stop," says Luke.

"But if you try sometimes," his father sings, "you just might find, you get what you need."

They walk to the edge of the parking lot. The road goes

nowhere in both directions.

"What're we going to do for five hours?" asks Luke.

A big tractor trailer pulls out of the parking lot, revealing a white sign posted by the road:

KLACK BROS. MUSEUM
15 MILES NORTH

His father sees it too. "I love it," he murmurs. "Klack Brothers Museum. I wonder what kind of stuff they have there?"

"It's probably farm equipment." He's been dragged to such places on school field trips.

"I can take you, if you like," says a voice behind them. It's a man in a pickup, the window rolled down. "I'm going up there." He jerks a thumb at the back of his truck, which is filled with plastic-wrapped cases of drinks and chocolate bars. "I supply their snack bar. It's only a fifteen-minute drive."

Luke fake smiles and looks to his father to make an excuse. But his father says, "You're sure it's no trouble?"

"No trouble."

Luke stares, silent with surprise, at his father. His father is not impulsive by nature, but lately he's been doing uncharacteristic things. Long walks at night. Swimming. Trying to teach himself guitar. He says these things are meant to "unlock" himself.

"What about the train?" Luke reminds him.

"We've got five hours," Dad replies. "You keep telling me how bored you are. Let's go see something new."

"They've got some real interesting things up there," says the driver.

"How would we get back?" his father asks, with more of his characteristic caution.

"I'll be there a couple hours. I do their plumbing too. I'm coming back this way if you want to catch a ride with me."

"Sounds perfect," says Dad.

It rises from the empty prairie like a mirage, a perfect little village of stone buildings and fences and barns.

"Weirdest thing, isn't it?" says their driver. "These two brothers, they came out from England about a hundred forty years ago and they ran a circus for a while. Then they decided to build a village in the middle of nowhere. They built a big manor house for themselves, and a school house. There was a racetrack and a cheese-making shop and some livestock, and they waited for people to come.

But the railway built too far to the south and wouldn't give them a spur line. So after a while it became a ghost town. One of the relatives turned it into a museum about fifteen years ago."

Luke has a sinking feeling there will be old ladies in white caps and pleated dresses telling him how to churn butter. Odd, slow-talking men in barns will show him how rope is made. If he's lucky a blacksmith will bang on a horseshoe.

"Incredible story," Luke's father says, looking around.

His father and the driver make small talk. They drive through a gate and pull up outside a little cottage with a thatched roof. A sign says, Tickets Snacks Gifts. Luke can't help noticing that there are only three other cars in the entire parking lot.

"You'll get your tickets in here," says the man. "And I'll be leaving about five o'clock."

"Thanks very much," Luke's father says. "Much obliged."

Luke winces. He can't believe his father just said "much obliged."

"Maybe there's a cowboy hat you can buy," Luke says as they walk in.

His father gives him a withering look.

White plastic tables and chairs are scattered around the

room. A few shelves display dismal local history books with black-and-white photos of fields on the covers. There is a Coke machine and a rack with some chips and chocolate bars on it. An elderly man behind the counter greets their driver.

"Afternoon, Wilfred."

"Uriah. I brought these folks up from the train." Their driver turns to them. "This is Uriah Klack. He owns the place."

Uriah turns his attention to Luke and his father—staring hardest at Luke.

"We'd like to see the museum," Luke's father says cheerfully.

"How old's the boy?" Uriah asks.

"Fourteen."

"Twenty dollars, please."

Uriah Klack reminds Luke a bit of Grandpa before he died: tall, like his bones are too big for his skin. His face is a bit sunken in, and his cheekbones stand out like knobs of shiny, polished wood. His knuckles bulge.

"You'll want to start in the manor house," says Uriah Klack. "Turn right out the doors."

Flanking the gravel drive to the big house are rows of carts and ploughs and farm machinery so dull that Luke doesn't even bother to pause. His father casts a steady eye over it all—as if it means anything to him. His father's never so much as planted a carrot seed.

"This would be the big plough," his father says in the solemn tones of a museum guide, "and next to it here, the *medium*-sized plough. . . ."

Luke grins. "And then we come to the rusty, broken-down plough. . . ."

"The first tractor used on the farm. . . ."

"And this would be the barbed wire collection."

There's something a little frightening about the way it's all displayed neatly on a plywood board, all the different types of lethal knots labeled.

"Some very fine samples," Luke says solemnly.

"An excellent collection," his father concurs.

They laugh together. It's one of the first times in days. This isn't so bad, Luke thinks. He can tell his friends about the lamest museum ever when he gets back.

The manor house is an impressively large stone pile. The lower floor is all trestle tables covered with little things. To Luke it looks like a school craft fair: miniature carts and horses, model farm buildings and general stores with ancient tinned goods arranged around them. There are Native dolls interspersed with Disney toys, an ancient cash register, a worker's time clock. The village is ghostly with all its frozen dolls and wooden people—like things that were stolen from a century of dead children.

"Is there anything they *didn't* collect?" Luke wonders aloud.

"Stamps. I don't think I've seen any stamps."

"It's not really a museum at all, is it?" Luke whispers.

His father shakes his head.

"It's just a bunch of stuff."

Luke heads upstairs alone and meanders down the main hallway. Most of the rooms are cordoned off, and you can look inside at the furniture: a bed, a dresser with a washbasin atop it, a rolltop desk and chair, musty old books on top. There are lots of mannequins dressed in period clothing. The plaster is chipped on their faces and hands, and some of their limbs don't seem to connect properly, sticking out at awkward angles, making them seem restless.

Luke keeps checking the time on his phone. He doesn't want to miss their ride back to the station. There's not even reception out here. He passes only one other family, and the girl looks as bored as he does. They stare numbly at each other in mute sympathy. As lame as the train is, the idea of being stranded out here is even worse.

When he enters a large parlor, his eyebrows lift with

interest. It's set up like a circus sideshow, divided into many stalls with tattered but colorful posters over each one: "Cordelia the Human Snake!" and "The Cardiff Giant!" and "The Indestructible Heart!" Eagerly, Luke moves from stall to stall. The human snake is a disappointment, just some big scraps of snakeskin crudely sewn together into a torso. The Cardiff Giant is more impressive—a huge body encased in a stone slab. It reminds Luke of those fossilized people they recovered from Pompeii after the volcano erupted. The indestructible heart is the creepiest of all. It floats inside a big tank of murky water. It looks pretty real to Luke, plump and moist. A little card underneath reads: "The heart of poet Percy Shelley, which remained undamaged even after the body was cremated! Sometimes it gives a beat!"

At the far end of the sideshow is a windowless wooden shack. A sign over the door says: "Ghost Boy."

Luke tries the door and finds it locked.

"That's extra," says Uriah Klack, appearing suddenly to Luke's right. He smells like clean laundry and cough drops.

"What's the ghost boy?" Luke asks.

"That's my star attraction. It's two dollars, just a little extra. I'll let you both in for three."

Luke looks over to see his Dad approaching.

"Sounds like a deal," his father says.

Luke's pretty sure it'll just be another ancient mannequin, but he feels a haunted-house thrill as Mr. Klack unlocks the door with his shaky hand. His father winks at him. He passes through the doorway. A single bulb casts pale red light through a Chinese lantern. Incense can't quite hide the smell of mildew.

There is a black lacquered chest against one wall, with many small square drawers. Chinese ginger jars are arranged on its surface, along with an incense burner, some kind of writing board, and ink brushes. The scattered plastic toys—a car, a helicopter—seem out of place. Tacked up are pictures of the Great Wall of China and mountains, looking like they were torn from calendars or magazines. In the middle of the room is a stool with a red cushion.

"There's no one in here," Luke says, but just hearing himself say it makes the hairs on his forearm lift.

"Maybe he's on break," his father chuckles.

"He's there on the stool," says Mr. Klack.

Luke stares. "I can't see anything."

"Don't look right at him," says Mr. Klack. "Look off to the side for a bit."

Luke does so. In his peripheral vision, a smudge appears atop the stool. He glances over quickly, and it disappears.

He looks off again, and this time the smudge gains definition and sharpens into limbs and a torso and the head of the Chinese boy, about his age.

"Do you see it?" he asks his Dad.

"That's a clever trick. Some kind of video projection."

Luke glances overhead for a ceiling-mounted projector or a dusty beam of light. There's nothing up there he can see. He studies the boy on the red-cushioned stool, staring sadly at the wall. He's dressed in drab canvas trousers and a jacket. The collar and buttons look old-fashioned.

"That's a nice seat he has there, eh?" says Mr. Klack. "We had an armchair for him a while back, but he seems to like the stool better."

The ghost boy taps the heel of one of his scuffed shoes against the rung—it's the only part of him that's moving. His chest doesn't rise and fall. But then his head turns and Luke knows he's looking at him. Luke takes a few steps to one side, and the ghost boy's head turns to follow. How's this trick managed? It seems way too sophisticated for old Mr. Klack and his half-hearted museum.

"We take good care of him," says Uriah Klack. "All sorts of familiar things from his own country."

"Those are actually Indonesian," Dad says, pointing at a pair of shadow puppets nailed to the wall. It's the kind of thing Dad knows.

"Yep," says Mr. Klack, nodding. "Just wanted to make him feel right at home."

"Hello," Luke says to the ghost boy, curious to know the limits of this illusion.

"Doesn't talk much," says Mr. Klack. "Not since I've had him. My father said he used to talk sometimes. Probably got discouraged. Anyway, he only knows Chinese."

Well, that's convenient, Luke thinks.

"You've never had anyone here who speaks Chinese?" Luke's father asks. Luke looks over, wondering if his father's just playing along. Surely he doesn't think it's real.

"In Meadows? We don't get many people out here," Klack says.

The ghost boy opens his mouth and says something, so softly Luke can't hear.

"See?" says Mr. Klack excitedly. "He's trying to say something to you. I had a feeling he'd talk to you. You'd be about the same age. Listen! he might try again!"

The ghost boy's lips part and he speaks once more. Luke thinks he makes out a foreign language.

"I don't know what he said." Luke feels frustrated—he senses he's being made a fool of and he doesn't like it. But his skin is prickly with the possibility this is real.

Luke sees his father walking all around the Chinese boy, studying him from different angles. He reaches out a hand.

"He doesn't like being touched," Mr. Klack says simply.

"Is that right?" Luke's father replies.

"There's this thing he does," Mr. Klack adds.

Luke's father touches the ghost boy on the shoulder—and pulls his hand back quickly with a pained grunt.

"What?" Luke asks in alarm.

His father is moving his lips and tongue around like he has a terrible taste in his mouth. He pulls a tissue from his pocket and spits into it. "It's like having aluminum foil crammed into your mouth!"

"Are you serious?"

"Told you," Mr. Klack says.

"It's not real," Luke blurts out, a little scared now. "Dad?"

"So how did you come into possession of a ghost?" Luke's father asks, ignoring his son.

Luke can't tell if his father's just having a joke with Mr. Klack. He wants to bolt from the room, but he's transfixed by Mr. Klack's voice.

"He was in my great-grandfather's collection. From the circus days. Uriah had all sorts of freaks and oddities in his show, and he was very proud of his ghost boy. Exhibited him across the country. You see that handbill there?"

He points to a small framed poster on the wall, advertising the Klack Bros. Circus. There's so much text on the poster, it takes Luke a moment to find it: "The Ghost Boy of Peking!"

"There's no end to the things he collected," Mr. Klack continues. "I'm still digging it all out from the attics and barns, labeling it real careful." He nods at the ghost boy. "He was just a jar of ash. I was about to throw it out when I saw him. He comes with the ashes, you see."

Mr. Klack nods at a slim jar atop the chest of drawers.

"His actual ashes are in there?" Luke asks.

"Can't go far from it," says Mr. Klack.

"Why's it tied to the wall?" Luke's father wants to know.

"He tries to shake it off the shelf sometimes," Mr. Klack remarks.

"I see," Luke's father says solemnly.

"Why're you talking like you believe this?" Luke demands.

When his father looks at him, Luke knows he's not joking. Luke can't stand it a second longer. He steps forward and puts his hand on the ghost boy's shoulder. Cold numbs his fingers. He sees a mountain, feels its ice-cold breath. Workers with tools step toward a hole in the rock face, and a terrible sensation of dread wells from it—and that's all, because Luke pulls back, terrified.

"He was talking to you, wasn't he?" says Mr. Klack, his

eyes shining with expectation. "I heard him talking!"

"Luke, what happened?" His father has a hand on his back.

"I . . . saw some pictures. People on a mountain." He wants a drink, something to wash the taste of soot and desolation from his mouth.

"He's never done that with anyone before," says Mr. Klack. "I've been worried about him lately. I think he gets lonely."

"He is lonely," Luke murmurs. How else to explain that dreadful windswept cold that passed through him?

"But he seems to like you," says Mr. Klack. "What I'm saying is he could use some company. A boy his own age."

"What?" Luke says, shaking his head. He has a swimmy feeling of unreality.

"He's getting faint. I don't want him fading away altogether. I'll give you a good price," Mr. Klack says to Dad.

Dad looks confused for a moment and then laughs. "Hell, I'll let you have him for free." He claps a hand on Luke's shoulder. Luke shrugs it off.

"No, sir, that won't do. It's got to be a fair price. I'm a fair dealer. How about a hundred dollars?"

Again his father chuckles, though more guardedly. "I think I'll hold on to him a little while longer."

"I'm joking," says Mr. Klack. When he smiles all the hollows and peaks of his face are exaggerated into a puppet mask.

Luke still hasn't adjusted to a world in which there are ghosts—and isn't sure he wants to. He needs to get out of this room, to forget everything that's happened. He pushes past his father and leaves. Mr. Klack comes after him.

"You sure you don't want to talk to him some more?"

"I wasn't *talking* to him." Where's his father? He wants this creepy Klack person away from him.

"But he showed you something. He was showing you things."

"I didn't like it," Luke murmurs.

"There's probably other things he'd show you."

"I didn't like it!" Luke says more loudly. "Dad!"

His father emerges from the room. "We should get going."

"Well, it's a shame we can't let these two have more time together," says Mr. Klack, his brow furrowed. "I'd like to know what that boy's story is."

"Good-bye," Luke's father says to Mr. Klack.

As he moves down the hallway, Luke's aware of Mr. Klack watching them, just standing there staring. He wants to run, but his father is beside him, walking steady, though there's a tense expression on his face. In movies, men like Mr. Klack unexpectedly produce deboning knives, or needles filled with lethal drugs.

When they emerge from the manor house, Luke sees the pickup that had brought them turning down the gravel drive toward the highway. His father gives a yell and waves his arm, running after it a few steps, but he's too late, and the truck disappears around the corner. Luke's heart starts to pound. His father never does stuff like this. He hates making a scene.

"We'll call a taxi," his father says, dragging out his cell phone.

"There's no reception," Luke says dully, wondering if there's even a taxi in a place like this.

His father persists, holding his phone out every which way.

"There's a payphone by the snack shop," Luke says. He remembers because you hardly ever see them now. "Dad, are we okay?"

His father's jogging toward the snack shop, Luke hurrying after. "Of course. I just don't want to miss the train."

"That wasn't a real ghost," Luke says, wanting his father to agree, to explain, but he doesn't say anything. They reach the pay phone, and his father snatches up the receiver.

"Do you have coins?" he asks Luke. "It doesn't take

credit cards." Luke notices his father glance back at the manor house. There's no one there.

Luke gives him a couple of quarters. His father's hand shakes slightly as he puts them into the slot.

"That guy was creepy," Luke says. "Wanting to buy me!"

"It was a joke," says his father.

The quarters come right out the bottom. His father tries again, and then with assorted nickels and dimes. They all come out.

"Maybe the operator will connect you, since the machine's broken," he tells his father.

His father presses zero and frowns. "It's very staticky . . . hello? Hello? Can you . . . hello?" Eventually, after a bit more shouting, he hangs up. "They can't hear me."

"What're we going to do?" Luke asks.

He imagines them running down the gravel drive, out onto the road, trying to flag down traffic. There are only two cars in the parking lot, and Luke's willing to bet the ancient farm truck belongs to Mr. Klack.

"Hello!" comes a distant voice, and Luke looks up to see Mr. Klack calling out from a second-story window of the manor house. "I need to talk to you!"

"I don't want to talk to him," Luke whispers.

"Me neither," says his father.

From one of the barns comes the family Luke saw earlier. They're walking toward the parking lot, in the direction of an SUV with North Dakota plates. That must be them. His father's already walking toward them.

"Excuse me," he says, smiling. "My son and I missed our ride back to the train station. We're passengers on the Canadian. Are you heading through Meadows by any chance?"

Luke notices the man look at his wife, uncertain. She hesitates. They both glance at him. Luke tries to look as harmless as possible.

"Um, okay," says the man.

"Thank you so much," says Luke's dad. "My name's Paul Morrow, and this is my son, Luke. We're from Toronto."

His father strikes up an amiable chatter, to prove they're not criminals or psychopaths. Luke keeps an eye on the manor house, watching the empty window where Mr. Klack's head appeared. They reach the car, and Luke climbs into the backseat with his father and the girl, who doesn't look very happy to be sharing her domain. They've just slammed their doors when Mr. Klack emerges from the manor house. He's walking with a stiff, quick-legged gait, arms waving.

The car engine muffles his words, but Luke thinks he

hears, "Hold up! Hold up there!"

The driver slows down. "Does he want to talk to you?" he asks Luke's father.

"I think he's just waving good-bye," Luke's father says, waving enthusiastically. "He's a bit eccentric. Did you talk to him?"

The man looks uncertainly but keeps going. Mr. Klack is still hobbling down the drive, waving and shouting. All Luke's muscles are clenched, and he's holding his breath. He doesn't exhale until they're through the gate and turning onto the highway back to Meadows.

In the dining car, Luke eats hungrily. His father seems distracted. They haven't really said much about the Klack Bros. Museum, like they can barely believe it happened. Already it seems far away, disappearing over the horizon like the train station they left an hour ago.

He eats some more mashed potatoes and looks out the window. Fields roll past in the last light of day. He stops chewing. In the reflection he sees someone sitting beside him. He turns and looks at the empty seat. His forearms course with electricity.

"Dad?" he whispers.

"I see him too."

Luke stares straight ahead and sees the faint ghost boy in his peripheral vision, looking at him. His foot taps noiselessly against the leg of his chair.

"Why is he here?"

Luke looks around the dining car. No one else has noticed the ghost boy. He's just a pale smudge in the brightly lit car, easily dismissed.

"There's something he wants to tell you maybe," Dad says quietly.

Luke can't believe they're talking like this. Like it's all true and this is really happening. He feels the presence of the ghost like a cold weight in his stomach. He puts down his fork.

"I don't get it. How's he here? Mr. Klack said he stays with his ashes, and his ashes are in the museum."

His father says nothing. He reaches into his jacket pocket and lifts out the slim jar.

Luke stares, horrified. "Mr. Klack put it in your pocket?"

"I took it."

Luke's not hungry anymore. As they walk back to their cabin, his head feels like it's filled with TV static. Inside, his father locks the door.

"Why?" Luke asks.

His reply is simple. "He's got a story."

"You stole the ghost!"

"No one else'll ever have a story like this."

"You *stole*—"

"How can you *steal* a ghost?" his father says impatiently. "It doesn't belong to anybody. You can't *own* a ghost. All I want is his story."

"He can't tell his story!"

"He'll tell *you*. You had a rapport with him."

From the corner of his eye, Luke can see the ghost boy sitting at the edge of his bunk, staring at him forlornly.

"He *wants* to tell you something," his father says. "It's you he keeps looking at."

"*You* get his story," Luke says.

"He doesn't talk to me. I tried again." He winces, remembering.

"I don't want to touch him," Luke says. "It doesn't feel good. It scares me."

"There's nothing to be scared of. . . ."

Luke laughs. "How would you know? You know all about ghosts?"

"Aren't you even curious?" His father sniffs dismissively. "Or maybe you're not interested in anything."

"It's not my fault you're blocked," Luke says angrily. "Think up your own stories."

He grabs the pillow off his bunk, and his winter coat.

"What are you doing?" his father demands.

"I'm not sleeping in the same cabin as him," Luke says. *Or you*, he thinks. "I'd rather sleep in the dome car."

It's late and the train is quiet. It's off season and there aren't many passengers aboard—and most of them are so old they're probably already asleep. On his way to the rear of the train, he passes lots of empty berths. Who would want to take the train anyway?

He climbs the stairs to the empty dome car. The lights are off and he has an amazing view of the stars. In the distance he can see the darker shadow of the approaching Rockies. He's glad he's brought his coat. He tries to get comfortable in his seat, but it doesn't even recline. He half expects his father to come after him, but he doesn't.

Luke is desperate to lie down and sleep. He leaves the dome car and starts walking forward to his cabin. He passes one of the porters having a cigarette, blowing his smoke out a little window between the cars. He nods to Luke as Luke passes. Luke doesn't want to go back to the cabin, and when he passes yet another empty berth, he wonders if anyone would know if he took one. He checks for the porter then slips inside. He zips up the thick curtain, stretches out, and is soon asleep.

But he's aware of not sleeping well, and being cold. He wakes in darkness, shivering. Beyond the window, a moon hangs over the hills. In the splash of silver light he sees the ghost boy hunched at the end of his berth, knees drawn up to his chin.

Luke backs up against the wall, his hand knocking against something hard. The jar of ashes. His father must have put it there. He looks at the curtain of his berth and sees it's slightly unzipped. His father *put* it in here with him—like locking him in a cage with a wild animal! What was he hoping? That Luke would get the ghost's story? He starts to fumble his way out of the berth, but he catches sight of the ghost boy, eyes wide with grief—and hope. Luke hesitates.

"What do you want?" he whispers.

Urgently, the boy says something that Luke can't hear.

"I can't hear you—"

But the ghost boy just keeps talking.

"Stop, stop," Luke says in frustration and pity. "It's not working." He chews his lip. He looks out the window.

Then he reaches out and puts his hand on the boy's shoulder.

The cold pulls him in. There is a mountain and a work camp cut into the cliff. An old-fashioned locomotive steams impatiently at the end of the line while men—white, Chinese—unload steel rails. Luke feels himself moving toward a gash blasted into the side of the cliff, and then he's inside, descending with a group of men. Darkness squeezes him. At the end of the tunnel men drill holes, inserting wads of explosives. Then the men all rush back, crouch behind barriers. There is a terrible sound, and smoke and grit boil past. The ground stops shaking. The smoke begins to clear. Men are standing. Without warning, a second explosion bowls them over, and a thunderclap comes from the ceiling before it collapses.

Luke pulls his hand back and shakes it to get the circulation going. His heart is racing.

"You worked on the railway," he whispers to the ghost boy. He studied it last year in school. They had to blast through the mountains to lay the tracks. Thousands of Chinese worked the most dangerous jobs, for half what the white men made. "Is that how you died? In a blast?"

The Chinese boy looks at him solemnly, expectantly. Luke reaches out again.

Broken bodies are laid on the ground. Even though the boy's body has been burned and crushed, Luke recognizes it. It's nighttime. A man steps among the corpses, examining them quickly, then lifts the boy's limp body over his shoulder. Luke floats after him into the woods. A second man meets the first. Money changes hands. The second man sews the body into a sack, loads it onto the back of a cart, and drives off down a rutted mountain road.

"That doesn't look right," Luke mutters, pulling back his hand and blowing warm breath onto it. "Why'd they take your body?"

He knows the only way to get the answer. He touches the boy's shoulder again.

A big bonfire burns. The sack is added to the flames. A man watches from the fire's edge. His wide-brimmed hat hides his face. He's reading from a large book. The sack burns away and the body is reduced to coarse gray ash. The man bends down and collects the ash into a jar. Luke feels like he himself is being squished into that jar, shoulders jammed in, head pushed roughly down, his body no longer his own, his will broken. The moment the stopper is sealed on top, blackness wraps itself around him—

—and is ripped away to give a view of bars, and people staring in at him: men laughing, women holding hands over their mouths in fear, a child crying and tugging at a father's hand. Luke feels utterly defeated and hopeless.

On the wall, high out of reach, is the jar of ashes.

Luke drags his numb hand away, panting. "They burned

your body and . . . *made* you a ghost."

The ghost boy points excitedly out the window. Luke cups his hands against the glass and peers out at the mountains spiking the sky. Close beside the tracks, a dark river runs between snowy banks. He looks wonderingly back at the ghost boy.

With great effort, the boy raises his arm and mimes throwing something to the floor.

"You want me to break the jar?" Luke says.

The boy does it again, more emphatically, then points out the window.

To Luke it can only mean one thing. The ghost boy wants to be released, outside, in the mountains where he died.

"Yes," Luke says, "I will."

He pulls his shoes on and unzips his berth. He needs to find a window he can open. The ones in the cabin don't, not in the dome car either. Then he remembers the porter, smoking. He grabs the jar and heads for the back of the car.

From the berth, a big-knuckled hand darts out and grabs his wrist. Luke gives a strangled cry as Uriah Klack's bony head protrudes from the curtains.

"I need my boy back."

Luke tries to pull free, but the old man's grip is like a metal claw.

"Let me go or I'll yell!" Luke croaks.

"Shhhh," Mr. Klack hisses. "Now then. You give me the jar back. You've stolen from me."

"I didn't steal anything!"

"I could call the police. You don't want your dad to go to jail, do you?"

"You're the one's going to jail," Luke says, "for keeping him prisoner."

"I'm not keeping him prisoner," Mr. Klack says in astonishment, his grip still tight.

"He's like a slave! You just make money off him."

"I'm taking *care* of him."

"You don't own him," Luke says. "You can't *own* someone."

"He isn't a someone, he's a *ghost*. And he's been the property of my family for over a hundred years."

"He wants to be free!"

"Is that what he told you?" Mr. Klack sits up and swings his bony legs off the berth.

"Yes!"

"I wouldn't go believing what a ghost tells you, son. They'll tell you all sorts of things. You don't want to go letting that ghost out of the jar. Ghosts can do terrible things if you set them free."

From the corner of his eye, Luke is aware of the ghost boy, watching him mournfully.

"See those big, sad eyes of his," Mr. Klack says. "Don't be fooled. He wants revenge."

"Not on me!" Luke says, and wrenches his arm back so hard Mr. Klack spills off the berth onto the floor. Luke twists free. He feels bad leaving an old man on the floor, until he sees Mr. Klack spring up with a speed far beyond spry.

"You give my boy back now," he says, hurrying after Luke.

Luke bolts down the length of the car to its end. The window there has a complicated latch, and it takes him a moment to figure it out. He opens it. Cold wind swirls in. He lifts the jar to throw. Mr. Klack grabs his other arm and pulls him away from the window. The jar falls from Luke's hand. It hits the floor and the top cracks open. A bit of gray ash spills out. Mr. Klack gives a gasp and steps away like it might burn him.

From the corner of his eye, Luke sees the ghost boy smiling.

Luke snatches up the jar and hurls it out the window. For a second it catches the moonlight as it curves toward the river, and then he can't see it anymore.

He turns and looks at Mr. Klack triumphantly, but he feels like crying. The old man says nothing, just wipes a big hand across his face and walks off.

When Luke returns to the cabin, his father sits up in his bunk and turns on the light. He looks at his son expectantly.

"Invent your own stories," Luke says, climbing into his own bunk and facing the wall.

It takes him a long time to fall asleep. When he finally does, he's thinking of the black river beside the tracks. The water would carry the ashes down through the mountains, through slow curves and surging gorges, to the sea.

THE WARLORDS OF RECESS
BY ERIC NYLUND

Commander Kane looked from the bridge of his mighty warship, *Colossus*.

The central view screen showed a blue planet swirled with clouds. A world called "Earth." Its defenses would only take a minute to annihilate. Then it would be known as "colony world 4729-B."

Commander Kane smoothed his neat iron-gray beard, brushed imaginary lint from the sleeve of his black uniform, and adjusted the campaign ribbons making a rainbow over his chest.

He nodded to his weapons crew to begin.

Ten junior officers straightened at their stations. Their

eager faces were lit from the nearby computers that showed missiles armed and a fleet of invasion craft ready to launch.

Rule Officer Lieutenant Plagen cleared his throat.

Commander Kane grimaced. This happened *every* single time. He held up a hand to signal the weapon officers to halt.

Lieutenant Plagen wore a white uniform with gold buttons that should have made him stand out among the rest of the crew. Yet he had the uncanny ability to sneak up on the commander.

"Yes, Lieutenant Plagen?" Commander Kane asked.

"Sir." Plagen snapped a crisp salute. "Rule 039? I'm sure you *meant* to give the order." He arched one eyebrow, knowing very well the commander hadn't. "It is my duty to remind the commander that *The Test* must be given to any world about to be conquered by the Eternal Empire."

"Rule 039," Commander Kane muttered. "Of course."

The Empire spanned the galaxy. It ruled four hundred colony worlds and would last forever because of its rules— all 33,452 of them.

The Commander secretly thought most of those rules could be ignored and no one would notice.

Except, that is, the Rules Officer required to go on every mission.

Which was *another* rule.

Commander Kane exhaled. He turned to his intelligence officer.

She anticipated his order, leaned over her instruments, and scanned the planet Earth.

"Detecting several military bases, sir," she told him.

A smug smile appeared on Plagen's face.

Of course the Rules Officer was happy. He enjoyed these pointless, cruel tests.

"Very well," Commander Kane told his intel officer. "Find an easy target. I want to make this quick. No need to make these 'earthlings' suffer more than they must."

She nodded. "Filtering the results, sir."

Rule 039 was ancient—from before the Empire had traveled to the stars. It was from a time when they had respected their enemies. Honor and courage had meant more than pushing a button and bombing planets from orbit without fear of a real fight.

The rule tested their enemies.

The Empire sent three squads against a like number of enemy soldiers. If the enemy won these battles, then they were worthy of the Empire's respect. They would be called "friend," and the Empire would leave in peace.

It was a worthless exercise. Not since the Empire had

taken to the stars had anyone ever won a Rule 039 test.

"Found a likely candidate," the intel officer said, looking up from her scanners. "A training camp for young warriors. They are currently engaged in simulated battle drills. Something called 'recess.'"

"That sounds perfect," Rules Officer Plagen said. "What is the name of this place for the official record?"

"Evergreen Elementary School," the intel officer replied.

"Proceed then," Commander Kane ordered. "Send in Squad Alpha."

"Sir? Alpha?" the intel officer asked.

Alpha squad had the ship's best soldiers. They won *every* fight, no matter what it cost. They were also known for leaving few, if any, survivors on the battlefield.

"Nothing fancy," Commander Kane said. "Just take them out. Quick."

Josh and Tony sat on the sidelines of Evergreen Elementary's basketball court. It was a hot spring day. The smell of cut grass was thick in the air.

The boys would've given anything to be out there running, dribbling, and having a great time.

No. That wasn't true.

They knew they were better off sitting out the game.

They *wished* they could run and pass and have a great time at basketball like everyone else.

But Josh and Tony were total klutzes.

Their classmates thundered past them and left them coughing in a cloud of dust.

So basketball wasn't their game (neither was dodgeball or soccer). No big deal. Instead, Josh and Tony were great at chess and board games with tiny squads of men that captured military bases in historical battles. No one else in the entire school could beat them.

Instead of everyone thinking this was cool, though, it just got them picked last every time, for every sport.

And they never got put into play anymore. That was fine with them. The few times it'd happened they'd gotten bruised and scuffed and spent more time flat on their faces.

It was humiliating.

So was sitting here. They were on display as the *least* athletic kids in the sixth grade.

Josh scratched a "#" in the dirt with his filthy sneaker. "Tic-tac-toe?"

Tony pushed his glasses higher onto his nose. He sweated and his glasses were always slipping and covered with greasy fingerprints.

"What's the point?" Tony said. "We always tie. How about chess?"

"Takes too long to find rocks to make the pieces," Josh said.

Josh knew Tony was about to suggest they draw the pieces in the dirt, then erase them and redraw every time they made a move. Last time they tried that the other kids called a timeout, came over, and trampled what had been one of their best chess games ever.

"Let's just—"

Tony stared past Josh, ignoring him, eyes locked on the court.

Josh followed his gaze.

The game had stopped. Both basketball teams faced some new kids.

There were five newcomers.

Josh had never seen them before. He was sure. He would have remembered *these* kids.

The three guys and two girls were a foot taller than any other kid at Evergreen. They looked like bodybuilders, in shorts and tight T-shirts with "ALPHA" stenciled on them along with numbers, one through five. They all wore mirrored wraparound sunglasses.

"'Alpha' is the first letter in the Greek alphabet," Tony said.

"Whatever," Josh told him, annoyed because he *hadn't* known that. Tony was always showing off.

The new kids must've said something funny, because all ten ordinary kids on the court laughed.

The biggest new kid (one with a crooked nose that looked like it'd been broken a few times) looked deadly serious as he continued to talk to them. He had the number 1 on his shirt. He picked up the basketball.

The two teams on the court lined up against the newcomers.

"How can they all play?" Tony whispered. "It'd be *two* teams against *one.*"

Josh scooted to the edge of the bench, eager to see what would happen next. "Doesn't matter how big those other kids are," he said. "With two teams, our guys will just dribble the ball around them."

The leader of the new kids tossed the ball at the Evergreen teams.

Shawn, the best basketball player at school, caught it, bounced the ball, and passed it to his teammate Jordan.

That's when the new kids burst into action.

The new kids' leader, Number 1, sprinted toward Shawn—and tackled him!

Shawn didn't even have the ball anymore.

He went down in a heap. The big guy bounced off him,

and Shawn "whoofed" as the air blasted out of his chest.

The large kid rolled to his feet, ready for more.

Meanwhile, Shawn lay moaning, barely moving.

Josh and Tony jumped to their feet.

"That was a *total* foul," Josh called out.

Tony nodded, wide-eyed.

That was just the start.

The huge kids jammed down the court.

One of them pulled out a bazooka squirt gun with a huge plunger. She aimed for Jordan and fired.

A stream of green fluid splattered Jordan—who slipped and fell and struggled in a web of blue-green slime.

The rest of the new kids tackled other players. One boy got tossed off the field (thankfully into the gym pads stacked on the sidelines).

The remaining three standing basketball players stared at the mayhem—then turned and ran!

Or, at least, they *tried to* run.

Two got hit with those gigantic squirt guns and went down. The last guy got straight-armed into the ground by the captain of the new kids.

It'd taken ten seconds. Both Evergreen basketball teams were on the ground, stuck in green goo, or dazed and barely moving.

And the new kids hadn't even *touched* the basketball!

"They can't do that," Josh whispered.

"Yeah, but they kinda *did* do it," Tony whispered back.

"We need to get a teacher," Josh said.

Which is when the leader of the new kids, this Number 1 guy, turned to them. "You two," he said. His voice sounded like rumbling thunder.

"Us?" Josh squeaked.

"You are on the team, aren't you?"

"N-not exactly," Tony stammered. "I mean, I guess, technically, yes. But we're on the bench. We're not supposed to actually play."

Josh elbowed Tony. He wasn't making this better.

Too late.

The captain of the new kids grinned at them, revealing a mouthful of pointed *shark* teeth. "Good. Get out on the field. And then we can finish this battle."

Josh had to escape. He took two steps away from the basketball court and started to run.

But Tony was too slow. The new kids surrounded him.

Tony looked panicked. He turned to Josh like he was the only person in the world who could save him.

If Josh could just sprint to the classrooms and get a teacher . . . but these kids were seriously damaged in the head. Especially that one with his teeth filed to points. What kind of crazy person does that? He couldn't leave Tony alone with Shark Face.

He glanced at his classmates on the ground, tangled in webs of sticky green goo. Josh didn't think he'd get very far running anyway.

"Great," Josh muttered.

He marched back to Tony. The gigantic kids parted and let him stand with his friend, and then closed ranks.

Josh nodded to the center of the basketball court. "Let's get this over with."

Tony shook his head so hard his glasses almost flew off. "We—we can't," he sputtered.

"There a choice?" Josh asked.

Tony sighed.

The new kids kept Josh encircled as he stopped at the half-court line.

Yeah, Josh was scared out of his mind, but he was also *annoyed*. None of these new kids were where they were supposed to be. They didn't have anyone to face him for the toss-up.

The shark-toothed leader shoved the basketball into Josh's hands.

"Play," he demanded.

The new kids crouched, ready to pounce.

"So who's going to throw the ball for the toss-up?" Josh asked.

The leader shook his head, not understanding. "Play!"

Tony pushed his glasses up the bridge of his nose. "Don't you guys know how to play basketball? There are rules, you know."

Every one of the new kids suddenly stood up straight— no longer in "crush and destroy" mode. They all stared at Tony.

The leader looked apologetically at his team. "No one told us there were . . . *rules*." His gaze dropped to his sneakers.

Josh recognized the awkward reaction because *he* felt that way when he'd played basketball and did something stupid (which was every time).

Which gave him an idea.

"Rules," he murmured to Tony and elbowed him.

Tony shook his head, not getting it.

"Just follow my lead," Josh whispered.

Josh cleared his throat. "Yeah, there are *lots* of rules."

The gigantic kids all started as if someone had cracked a whip. There was definitely something going on here.

A grin spread over Josh's face. "You guys just broke about

a dozen of the *biggest* rules in basketball." He pointed out the leader. "Especially you, buddy!"

The color drained from the big kid's face. His sharp smile vanished.

The other big kids muttered and looked around, everywhere but at their leader. It was as if they were embarrassed to know him.

"I . . . I didn't know," their leader protested.

"That doesn't matter," Tony said, picking up on Josh's idea. "Rules are rules. You broke them, and there are penalties."

The leader hung his head. He looked as if Tony had just said he was about to be shot by a firing squad.

"Free throws," Josh told the leader. "That's the usual penalty for a foul." He counted the dazed and tangled kids on the basketball court. "I figure at least ten of them."

Josh marched to the free-throw line, bouncing the basketball along the way. He almost kicked it. *That* would have looked cool.

"And since we're the only ones left on the team," Josh said, "we'll take the shots."

The big kids didn't move.

"You guys have to line up on either side." Tony told them. "And just watch. No jumping in to mess up the shots. That's another rule."

The big kids gulped and lined up.

Their leader was the last to join them. "No one told me about the rules," he repeated to himself.

Josh stepped up to the free-throw line. He bounced the ball a few times to warm up. He wasn't any good at this.

He launched the ball—it *spang*ed off the backboard.

A miss.

The big kids shifted as if they wanted to jump and tackle Josh. They restrained each other, though.

They *really* had a thing about rules.

Tony got the ball and tossed it to Josh.

He threw again—missed.

And missed again.

And again!

Josh shook his head. He was such a spaz sometimes.

He took a deep breath and squinted at the net.

He tossed the ball.

This time it rolled along the rim . . . circled once . . . twice . . . and dropped inside.

Josh grinned.

He turned to Tony. "You want to try?"

"Sure!" Tony's face lit up. In the few games he'd ever gotten to play in, no one had ever given him the ball.

Josh bounced the ball to Tony and he went to the free-throw line.

He threw the ball.

It bounced off the rim.

He tried again. This time he *entirely* missed the backboard.

Josh chased down the ball and passed it back to him.

Tony wasn't bummed. He just took the ball in both hands, swung it between his legs, and chucked it up underhanded.

It swished through the net.

Tony jumped up and whooped.

He used the same stupid technique again—and another swish!

Tony did a war dance on the free-throw line.

The big kids glared and moved in like they wanted to tear Tony apart.

Josh was about to warn him to cut it out, but then a bell rang.

Tony stopped dancing. "That's it," he said. "That's the fifteen-minute bell. We're supposed to stop and clean up before lunch break ends."

"It's three to nothing," Josh declared. "We, uh . . . won."

The big kids stared at them and their mouths dropped

open in astonishment.

Each had those weird shark teeth. Josh squinted. They didn't look fake, either. How could they be real?

Their faces twisted with barely contained rage. Jaws jutted out at sharp angles.

Something was really *off* with these kids.

One with the number 2 on her shirt tore the wraparound sunglasses off her face, crushed them in a fist, and tossed the remains. "You've won *this* battle," she said. "But it's not over. Our honor *will be* avenged."

Josh and Tony stared at each other.

There was a flash of light on the court. Another at the far end of the playground.

The lights left them both blinking, eyes filled with tears.

When they were able to see clearly again, the big kids had vanished. Except the leader. He stood by the free-throw line, his head hung low.

"What just happened?" Tony asked.

Josh shook his head. He went to their leader. "Why'd they leave you?"

"I have dishonored my squad," he whispered. "We have lost. By the rules, I am your captive now."

"Captive?!" Josh said. "What *are* you talking about?"

Tony yanked on Josh's arm. "Hey, look."

"Just a sec. I gotta ask this guy what—"

"No, seriously," Tony said, his voice rising.

Josh turned to tell Tony that this weird big kid was about to cry. That something was really, really wrong with today's recess. And that maybe they were about to find out why.

But the words stuck in Josh's throat.

He couldn't believe what he saw.

In the middle of the playground was a fort. It was made of plastic logs. Everyone loved to climb the thing. It was two levels high, and kids usually played a tag version of capture the flag during lunch.

Only at this very moment . . . there was a REAL battle happening.

Every kid at Evergreen Elementary out for lunch recess screamed and sprinted to the plastic log fort.

Everyone . . . except Josh and Tony (and the still-glued basketball teams stuck on the court).

Thirty new big kids had appeared from nowhere. They were like the ones Josh and Tony had trounced at basketball. But these wore blue shorts and numbered T-shirts that read: BETA.

There was no way they went to *this* school. They were

huge enough to be in high school (or to be professional wrestlers!).

Any bit of them looking normal was gone too. Their faces were wide, jaws twice normal size. They all had snarling mouths full of shark teeth.

And unlike when they were "playing" basketball, this time they carried those snot squirt guns out in the open. They zapped Tony and Josh's classmates left and right.

Josh and Tony watched, stunned, as terrified kids tripped and fell over one another to get away.

Blango! Splat!

In the bark-filled play area, kids tried to rise from mucous cocoons. They fell face-first into the gunk. Gross!

Only a dozen kids made it to the fort. They climbed the walls and cowered inside.

Meanwhile the big kids made sure all the kids down *stayed* down. They shot them an extra two or three times with their weapons . . . leaving blobs of quivering, angry, snot-covered kids.

"What's going on?" Josh whispered, terrified.

He hadn't expected any answer, but he got one from the leader of the weird basketball team he and Tony had beaten.

"It's the second test," he told Josh. "You won the first."

He nodded to the basketball court. "This is the second test. If the Empire wins, we will be tied."

"Em-empire?" Tony sputtered. "Tied? For what?"

"Rule 039," the big kid replied as calmly as if he were talking about the weather. "The Empire tests primitive worlds before they conquer them. If these worlds can beat the Empire three times, they leave in peace."

Josh and Tony exchanged confused looks.

"I am Unit 1," the big kid said. "In the *highly likely* case that this world will lose, the Empire moves in. First they will take this school. Then they take the planet."

Josh mouthed to Tony, "*Take the planet?*"

Tony shrugged and made a "crazy" circle motion near his head.

Josh blinked. Whatever was going on—rule whatchamacallit or not—all he knew was he had to help the Evergreen kids. Somehow.

"I don't know what you're talking about," Josh said to Unit 1, "but you've got to help us stop those guys. You're on *our* team, right?"

Unit 1 stood taller, suddenly at military attention.

"Unit 1 ready for orders, sir!"

"Wow, neat," Tony said.

Josh and Tony huddled and drew a map in the dirt—as

if this were a board game. The kids were *X*s clustered in the fort. The attackers were *O*s. They had them surrounded. Arrows showed the *O*s moving in for the kill.

After a split second, Tony whispered, "So, what are the rules?"

"Don't be stupid," Josh hissed. "There are no rules. This is a battle!"

Josh thought about it a second. That might not be true. There *were* rules. Plenty of rules on the school playground. Every time he set foot in the flower beds some teacher was waiting for him, handing out demerits.

And these new kids might be ruthless, but they also seemed to have this thing about following rules.

"I've got a crazy idea," Josh said to Tony and motioned Unit 1 closer. "Just do what I do. Come on."

Unit 1 snapped off a crisp salute.

Tony didn't look sure, especially when Josh marched boldly onto the playground—straight for three new kids. They were zapping a helpless, snot-covered boy.

"Hey, you creeps!" Josh shouted.

The three turned. They had numbers, 7, 18, and 29, on their shirts. They aimed their guns at Josh, Tony, and Unit 1.

"You jumped off that wall." Josh pointed to the cinder

block wall near the library. It was four feet tall. Almost everyone climbed up and balanced on it during recess. Nearby was a sign that read: NO CLIMBING OR JUMPING OFF THE WALL.

"Yeah, it's against the rules," Tony added, picking up on the idea. He crossed his arms over his chest like teachers did when lecturing rule breakers.

Unit 1 gasped as if this were the worst thing in the world.

The three big kids looked at each other. "There are no such rules," Unit 29 snarled.

"Sign?" Tony pointed to the library wall. "It's right there."

The three squinted—then they looked totally shocked. They set down their guns and raised their arms.

"We were not told," Unit 18 whispered. "What is the penalty? Death? Cutting off our ears? Vaporization?"

Unit 1 nodded enthusiastically at all these suggestions.

"I'm afraid," Josh said, tapping his finger to his lip, "it's worse."

"You have to join *our* team," Tony told them.

The three looked stunned, then looked to Unit 1. But then they shrugged, picked up their guns, and marched over to Josh and Tony.

"Yes!" Tony said.

"Orders, sir?" Unit 18 asked Josh.

Orders? Josh had no idea what to do next. He was just making this up as he went along.

"Look!" Tony pointed.

A squad of five larger kids had concentrated their slimy fire on the left side of the fort.

Josh gulped. "They're going to paste everyone up there."

"Not that," Tony muttered and pointed lower. "*Where* they're standing."

The five stood smack in the middle of the flower beds. These were the same trampled daisies that had gotten Josh so much detention.

He jogged toward them. "Hey," he shouted. "You can't be there. . . ."

In a few minutes, Josh and Tony had rounded up thirty of the big kids—busting them for trampling flowers, spitting, and the unauthorized discharge of a snot gun in the hallway (Tony made up that last one, but these new kids were so clueless, and so terrified of breaking rules, they believed him).

The only holdouts left were in the corner of the playground: ten bigger kids by the toolshed. One had "00" printed on his shirt, and looked even bigger than Unit 1. That's where Josh and Tony had seen flashes of light before the major mayhem had started.

Josh moved closer and tried to yell at them—but they opened fire!

Globules of snot splattered on the ground near him. A strand got on Josh's sneaker. It was such strong glue that he couldn't pry his shoe off the concrete.

He had to leave it behind.

Tony, Josh, and their new gang retreated. (The sock on Josh's foot made smacky sounds.)

"If you're worried about your foot, sir," Unit 1 told Josh, "we have cleanup solvent on the ship."

"Forget my foot," Josh told him. "We need to get that last bunch."

"You guys have a ship?" Tony asked.

Unit 1 pointed at the sky. "We have many ships between this planet and your moon."

Josh wasn't sure what to believe. Unit 1 said they were being tested. Three battles they had to win or the planet would be conquered. How else to explain the sudden appearance of all these weird big kids?

Or maybe nearby Lakeside High School had let out early. But there was no way high school kids would be following rules.

No, alien invasion was the more likely thing.

So, that meant they had to win this fight or their school and the Earth were toast!

"Should we get the teachers?" Tony whispered.

"Sure." Josh gestured to the playground and the dozen kids struggling in snotty webs. "They'll come out here and get gooed like everyone else."

Unit 1 fidgeted. "The longer we wait, sir, the more soldiers will be sent down."

"Okay," Josh said. "Let's try this."

He gathered everyone around him and drew in the dirt.

"We'll have a squad run up the middle to distract those hooligans at the shed," he said. "Two smaller squads will go right and left. I'll lead one. Unit 1, you lead the other. A third bunch will go the long way and surprise those guys from behind. That one"—he pointed to Tony—"you lead."

Tony's eyes widened at this, but he smiled.

"It should be over," Josh explained, "before anyone gets into serious trouble."

"Good plan." Unit 1 handed Josh and Tony each one of the guns.

Josh took it reluctantly. He'd been taught that guns were dangerous and not to be handled by twelve-year-olds. This thing was heavier than he thought it would be. It dripped snot from the end. Yuck!

"Ready?" Josh said.

Tony, Unit 1, and the other big kids on their team nodded.

"Okay—go!"

A pack of big kids sprinted up the middle of the playground. They screamed and fired at the other kids by the shed.

The enemy fired back, well hidden behind cover.

The middle squad got plastered—literally plastered—to the concrete!

But they did their job. Josh's squads silently running up the sides were *completely* ignored by the shed kids.

But as soon as Josh got close enough to open fire, six new big kids swung around the corner of the shed and opened fire on him.

Josh took cover by the swing set, which got covered with sticky strands.

He shot back and splattered a nearby maple tree. A total miss.

He gritted his teeth. He was pinned down behind this stupid swing. His team was going to lose!

But just then Tony appeared out of nowhere—*behind* the shed.

The enemy kids wheeled around. Tony and his team shot first.

Blammo—splat—splorch!

The enemy squad was covered in goo, stuck *to* the shed, cursing and struggling, helpless.

Josh ran over to them.

Tony had already taken charge. "Where's this transporter thingy you guys used to get down here?" he asked the largest enemy kid, number 00.

"We'll never tell you," Unit 00 snarled. He glanced back to the shed he was stuck to.

Tony opened the shed door.

Inside were four steel pillars covered with blinking lights.

"What are you doing?" Josh asked Tony.

"Going to win that third battle *before* it starts," Tony said.

The five-minute bell rang. Lunch recess was almost over. There wasn't much time left to save the world.

Inside Josh trembled, but he somehow turned to the enemy kids stuck to the shed and told them, "So . . . take us to your leader."

Josh and Tony burst onto the bridge of the alien ship and opened fire!

Two minutes earlier they'd teleported up from the shed and tangled every guard they saw on the ship.

The crew never expected to see two kids leading a dozen

others, splattering everything that moved.

Josh had taken a black officer uniform to help blend in. (Actually, he just wore the jacket. The pants were too big and kept falling down.)

They strolled right up to the ship's bridge.

Josh, Tony, and their team gooed and splorched the seven-foot-tall officers working the bridge controls.

Their leader (Josh guessed he was the leader because his uniform was covered with ribbons and medals) was the last unstuck enemy left standing. He slowly looked around and raised his hands in surrender.

Tony whooped and did his victory dance.

Josh meanwhile stared out the wide view screen at Earth. The world was so beautiful from up here.

"I am Commander Kane of the Imperial Star Ship *Colossus*," the leader told them.

Josh practically dropped his gun. The commander's voice was ironclad, and Josh felt like saluting him.

Instead, he cleared his throat. "I'm Josh, sir," he said, "from Evergreen Elementary. And this is Tony."

Tony waved at him.

"As I understand it," Josh went on, "if we win three battles against you guys, you can't conquer Earth, right?"

Commander Kane looked to one officer in a white

uniform glued to the deck.

"No . . . ," the person in white muttered. "The Empire cannot be defeated. Not by two children!"

"Rule 049," Commander Kane told him. "Are you suggesting, Lieutenant Plagen, that we break *a rule*?!"

There was a long pause, then Plagen said, "No, we follow *all* the rules."

A smile flickered under the commander's beard, revealing three rows of extra-sharp shark teeth (that sent gooseflesh crawling up Josh's arms).

"We will go in peace, then," Commander Kane said to Josh and Tony. "Well fought, young warriors."

Josh and Tony whooped and gave each other a high-five.

Unit 1 beamed at them. "When is the next battle, sirs? Perhaps Lakeside High School?" He cracked his beefy fingers.

"Uh . . . I think," Tony said, "you and the other guys have to stay."

Unit 1 looked as if Christmas had been canceled.

"No—you don't understand," Josh said, suddenly feeling bad for the big guy. "*Our* rules say that once the battle is over you have to go back to *your* team."

There was no such rule, but how else to get Unit 1 to stay? And how could he ever explain to his mom that he had to bring a few dozen alien warriors to live in their basement?

"It was fun," Tony said, "but rules are rules." He held out his hand for Unit 1 to shake.

"We've got to go," Josh added. "Recess is almost over and we've got a *huge* mess to clean up."

Unit 1 stared at Tony's hand, puzzled, as if he were unsure whether to clasp it . . . or bite it. He finally shook the offered hand. "It has been an honor to fight on your team, sirs." He looked around the bridge, at the struggling, glued officers. "I'll see to it that you get a few cans of detangling spray to clean up your school. . . ."

A minute later, Josh and Tony had handed out the last can of detangle spray to the basketball team at Evergreen.

As soon as the mist from the can touched the alien goo, it turned the stuff to dust.

Almost everyone on the playground was back to normal—stunned and not having a clue what had just happened but normal.

Not one of the big alien kids was left. They all must have teleported back to their ships.

The final recess bell rang.

Josh and Tony trotted off to their fourth-period science class.

Tony looked up. "You think they'll ever come back?"

"No way," Josh said. "We won. According to their rules they have to leave us in peace."

"I don't know . . . ," Tony whispered. "That Plagen guy didn't sound too happy that we beat him."

"You worry too much," Josh said. "Those rules of theirs are like unbreakable laws. I'd bet you a bazillion dollars we've seen the last of them."

Josh looked down—almost stepping into the flower beds. He caught himself, stopped, and carefully set his foot down on the concrete path.

Whew. That was a close one.

Rules Officer Lieutenant Plagen tried to wipe the last of the congealed tangler fluid from his normally clean white uniform.

Ugh! He would have used the detangle spray, but it tarnished his medals. What a mess.

How was he going to explain to Imperial Headquarters that two children from an insignificant planet had defeated the Empire's best?

And by using the Empire's own rules!

He ground his pointed teeth (making a *screeeeeech*ing sound that he very much enjoyed).

Plagen would not let this happen.

He took out his datapad and scrolled through the Empire's rulebook. All 33,452 entries.

Two could play *this* game.

He'd find some rule that would let him come back to this planet one day . . . and then, his new lifelong enemies, Josh and Tony, would be sorry they'd "won."

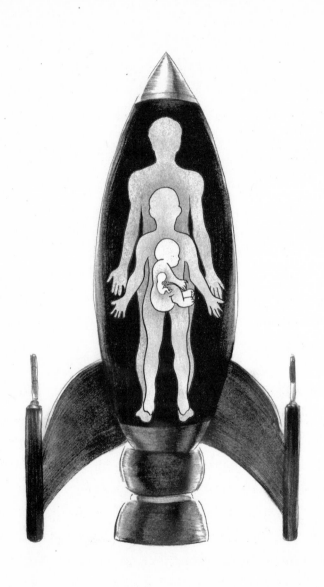

FROST AND FIRE
BY RAY BRADBURY

During the night, Sim was born. He lay wailing upon the cold cave stones. His blood beat through him a thousand pulses each minute. He grew, steadily.

Into his mouth his mother with feverish hands put the food. The nightmare of living was begun. Almost instantly at birth his eyes grew alert, and then, without half understanding why, filled with bright, insistent terror. He gagged upon the food, choked and wailed. He looked about, blindly.

There was a thick fog. It cleared. The outlines of the cave appeared. And a man loomed up, insane and wild and terrible. A man with a dying face. Old, withered by winds, baked like adobe in the heat. The man was crouched in a far corner of the cave, his eyes whitening to one side of his face, listening to the far wind trumpeting up above on the frozen night planet.

Sim's mother, trembling now and again, staring at the man, fed Sim pebble-fruits, valley-grasses and ice-nipples broken from the cavern entrances, and eating, eliminating, eating again, he grew larger, larger.

The man in the corner of the cave was his father! The man's eyes were all that was alive in his face. He held a crude stone dagger in his withered hands and his jaw hung loose and senseless.

Then, with a widening focus, Sim saw the old people sitting in the tunnel beyond this living quarter. And as he watched, they began to die.

Their agonies filled the cave. They melted like waxen images, their faces collapsed inward on their sharp bones, their teeth protruded. One minute their faces were mature, fairly smooth, alive, electric. The next minute a dessication and burning away of their flesh occurred.

Sim thrashed in his mother's grasp. She held him. "No, no," she soothed him, quietly, earnestly, looking to see if this, too, would cause her husband to rise again.

With a soft swift padding of naked feet, Sim's father ran across the cave. Sim's mother screamed: Sim felt himself torn loose from her grasp. He fell upon the stones, rolling, shrieking with his new, moist lungs!

The webbed face of his father jerked over him, the knife was poised. It was like one of those prenatal nightmares he'd had again and again while still in his mother's flesh. In the next few blazing, impossible instants questions flicked through his brain. The knife was high, suspended, ready to destroy him. But the whole question of life in this cave, the dying people, the withering and the insanity, surged through Sim's new, small head. How was it that he understood? A newborn child? Can a newborn child think, see, understand, interpret? No. It was wrong! It was impossible. Yet it was happening! To him. He had been alive an hour now. And in the next instant perhaps dead!

His mother flung herself upon the back of his father, and beat down the weapon. Sim caught the terrific backwash of emotion from both their conflicting minds. "Let me kill him!" shouted the father, breathing harshly, sobbingly. "What has he to live for?"

"No, no!" insisted the mother, and her body, frail and old as it was, stretched across the huge body of the father, tearing at his weapon. "He must live! There may be a future for him! He may live longer than us, and be young!"

The father fell back against a stone crib. Lying there,

staring, eyes glittering, Sim saw another figure inside that stone crib. A girl-child, quietly feeding itself, moving its delicate hands to procure food. His sister.

The mother wrenched the dagger from her husband's grasp, stood up, weeping and pushing back her cloud of stiffening gray hair. Her mouth trembled and jerked. "I'll kill you!" she said, glaring down at her husband. "Leave my children alone."

The old man spat tiredly, bitterly, and looked vacantly into the stone crib, at the little girl. "One-eighth of *her* life's over already," he gasped. "And she doesn't know it. What's the use?"

As Sim watched, his own mother seemed to shift and take a tortured, smokelike form. The thin bony face broke out into a maze of wrinkles. She was shaken with pain and had to sit by him, shuddering and cuddling the knife to her shriveled breasts. She, like the old people in the tunnel, was aging, dying.

Sim cried steadily. Everywhere he looked was horror. A mind came to meet his own. Instinctively he glanced toward the stone crib. Dark, his sister returned his glance. Their minds brushed like straying fingers. He relaxed somewhat. He began to learn.

The father sighed, shut his lids down over his green eyes. "Feed the child," he said, exhaustedly. "Hurry. It is almost dawn and it is our last day of living, woman. Feed him. Make him grow."

Sim quieted, and images, out of the terror, floated to him.

This was a planet next to the sun. The nights burned with cold, the days were like torches of fire. It was a violent, impossible world. The people lived in the cliffs to escape the incredible ice and the day of flame. Only at dawn and sunset was the air breath-sweet, flower-strong, and then the cave peoples brought their children out into a stony, barren valley. At dawn the ice thawed into creeks and rivers, at sunset the day fire died and cooled. In the intervals of even, livable temperature the people lived, ran, played, loved, free of the caverns; all life on the planet jumped, burst into life. Plants grew instantly, birds were flung like pellets across the sky. Smaller, legged animal life rushed frantically through the rocks; everything tried to get its living done in the brief hour of respite.

It was an unbearable planet. Sim understood this, a matter of hours after birth. Racial memory bloomed in him. He would live his entire life in the caves, with two hours a day outside. Here, in stone channels of air he would talk, talk incessantly with his people, sleep never, think, think and lie upon his back, dreaming; but never sleeping.

And he would live exactly eight days.

* * *

The *violence* of this thought! Eight days. Eight *short* days. It was wrong, impossible, but a fact. Even while in his mother's flesh some racial knowledge of some strange far wild voice had told him he was being formed rapidly, shaped and propelled out swiftly.

Birth was quick as a knife. Childhood was over in a flash. Adolescence was a sheet of lightning. Manhood was a dream, maturity a myth, old age an inescapably quick reality, death a swift certainty.

Eight days from now he'd stand half-blind, withering, dying, as his father now stood, staring uselessly at his own wife and child.

This day was an eighth part of his total life! He must enjoy every second of it. He must search his parents' thoughts for knowledge.

Because in a few hours they'd be dead.

This was so impossibly unfair. Was this all of life? In his prenatal state hadn't he dreamed of *long* lives, valleys not of blasted stone but green foliage and temperate clime? Yes! And if he'd dreamed then there must be truth in the visions. How could he seek and find the long life? Where? And how could he accomplish a life mission that huge and depressing in eight short, vanishing days?

How had his people gotten into such a condition?

As if at a button pressed, he saw an image. Metal seeds, blown across space from a distant green world, fighting with long flames, crashing on this bleak planet. From their shattered hulls tumbled men and women.

When? Long ago. Ten thousand days. The crash victims hid in the cliffs from the sun. Fire, ice and floods washed away the wreckage of the huge metal seeds. The victims were shaped and beaten like iron upon a forge. Solar radiations drenched them. Their pulses quickened, two hundred, five hundred, a thousand beats a minute. Their skins thickened, their blood changed. Old age came rushing. Children were born in the caves. Swifter, swifter, swifter the process. Like all this world's wild life, the men and women from the crash lived and died in a week, leaving children to do likewise.

So this is life, thought Sim. It was not spoken in his mind, for he knew no words, he knew only images, old memory, an awareness, a telepathy that could penetrate flesh, rock, metal. Somewhere along the line, they *had* developed telepathy, plus racial memory, the only good gifts, the only hope in all this terror. So thought Sim, I'm the five-thousandth in a long line of futile sons? What can I do to save myself from dying eight days from now? Is there escape?

His eyes widened, another image came to focus.

Beyond this valley of cliffs, on a low mountain lay a perfect, unscarred metal seed. A metal ship, not rusted or touched by the avalanches. The ship was deserted, whole, intact. It was the only ship of all those that had crashed that was still a unit, still usable. But it was so far away. There was no one in it to help. This ship, then, on the far mountain, was the destiny toward which he would grow. There was his only hope of escape.

His mind flexed.

In this cliff, deep down in a confinement of solitude, worked a handful of scientists. To these men, when he was old enough and wise enough, he must go. They, too, dreamed of escape, of long life, of green valleys and temperate weathers. They, too, stared longingly at that distant ship upon its high mountain, its metal so perfect it did not rust or age.

The cliff groaned.

Sim's father lifted his eroded, lifeless face.

"Dawn's coming," he said.

II

Morning relaxed the mighty granite cliff muscles. It was the time of the Avalanche.

The tunnels echoed to running bare feet. Adults, children pushed with eager, hungry eyes toward the outside dawn. From far out, Sim heard a rumble of rock, a scream, a silence. Avalanches fell into valley. Stones that had been biding their time, not quite ready to fall, for a million years let go their bulks, and where they had begun their journey as single boulders they smashed upon the valley floor in a thousand shrapnels and friction-heated nuggets.

Every morning at least one person was caught in the downpour.

The cliff people dared the avalanches. It added one more excitement to their lives, already too short, too headlong, too dangerous.

Sim felt himself seized up by his father. He was carried brusquely down the tunnel for a thousand yards, to where the daylight appeared. There was a shining insane light in his father's eyes. Sim could not move. He sensed what was going to happen. Behind his father, his mother hurried, bringing with her the little sister, Dark. "Wait! Be careful," she cried to her husband.

Sim felt his father crouch, listening.

High in the cliff was a tremor, a shivering.

"Now!" bellowed his father, and leaped out.

An avalanche fell down at them!

Sim had accelerated impressions of plunging walls, dust, confusion. His mother screamed! There was a jolting, a plunging.

With one last step, Sim's father hurried him forward into the day. The avalanche thundered behind him. The mouth of the cave, where mother and Dark stood back out of the way, was choked with rubble and two boulders that weighed a hundred pounds each.

The storm thunder of the avalanche passed away to a trickle of sand. Sim's father burst out into laughter. "Made it! By the Gods! Made it alive!" And he looked scornfully at the cliff and spat. "Pagh!"

Mother and sister Dark struggled through the rubble. She cursed her husband. "Fool! You might have killed Sim!"

"I may yet," retorted the father.

Sim was not listening. He was fascinated with the remains of an avalanche afront of the next tunnel. Blood trickled out from under a rise of boulders, soaking into the ground. There was nothing more to be seen. Someone else had lost the game.

Dark ran ahead on lithe, supple feet, naked and certain.

The valley air was like a wine filtered between mountains. The heaven was a restive blue; not the pale scorched atmosphere of full day, nor the bloated, bruised black-purple of night, a-riot with sickly shining stars.

This was a tide pool. A place where waves of varying and violent temperatures struck, receded. Now the tide pool was quiet, cool, and its life moved abroad.

Laughter! Far away, Sim heard it. Why laughter? How could any of his people find time for laughing? Perhaps later he would discover why.

The valley suddenly blushed with impulsive color. Plant life, thawing in the precipitant dawn, shoved out from most unexpected sources. It flowered as you watched. Pale green tendrils appeared on scoured rocks. Seconds later, ripe globes of fruit twitched upon the blade-tips. Father gave Sim to his mother and harvested the momentary, volatile crop, thrust scarlet, blue, yellow fruits into a fur sack which hung at his waist. Mother tugged at the moist new grasses, laid them on Sim's tongue.

His senses were being honed to a fine edge. He stored knowledge thirstily. He understood love, marriage, customs, anger, pity, rage, selfishness, shadings and subtleties, realities and reflections. One thing suggested another. The sight of green plant life whirled his mind like a gyroscope, seeking balance in a world where lack of time for explanations made a mind seek and interpret on its own. The soft burden of food gave him knowledge of his system, of

269

energy, of movement. Like a bird newly cracking its way from a shell, he was almost a unit, complete, all-knowing. Heredity and telepathy that fed upon every mind and every wind had done all this for him. He grew excited with his ability.

They walked, mother, father and the two children, smelling the smells, watching the birds bounce from wall to wall of the valley like scurrying pebbles and suddenly the father said a strange thing:

"Remember?"

Remember what? Sim lay cradled. Was it any effort for them to remember, when they'd lived only seven days!

The husband and wife looked at each other.

"Was it only three days ago?" said the woman, her body shaking, her eyes closing to think. "I can't believe it. It is so unfair." She sobbed, then drew her hand across her face and bit her parched lips. The wind played at her gray hair. "Now it is my turn to cry. An hour ago it was you!"

"An hour is half a life."

"Come." She took her husband's arm. "Let us look at everything, because it will be our last looking."

"The sun'll be up in a few minutes," said the old man. "We must turn back now."

"Just one more moment," pleaded the woman.

"The sun will catch us."

"Let it catch me then!"

"You don't mean that."

"I mean nothing, nothing at all," cried the woman.

The sun was coming fast. The green in the valley burnt away. Searing wind blasted from over the cliffs. Far away where sun bolts hammered battlements of cliff, the huge stone faces shook their contents; those avalanches not already powdered down were now released and fell like mantles.

"Dark!" shouted the father. The girl sprang over the warm floor of the valley, answering, her hair a black flag behind her. Hands full of green fruits, she joined them.

The sun rimmed the horizon with flame, the air convulsed dangerously with it, and whistled.

The cave people bolted, shouting, picking up their fallen children, bearing vast loads of fruit and grass with them back to their deep hideouts. In moments the valley was bare. Except for one small child someone had forgotten. He was running far out on the flatness, but he was not strong enough, and the engulfing heat was drifting down from the cliffs even as he was half across the valley.

Flowers were burnt into effigies, grasses sucked back

into rocks like singed snakes. Flower seeds whirled and fell in the sudden furnace blast of wind, sown far into gullies and crannies, ready to blossom at sunset tonight, and then go to seed and die again.

Sim's father watched that child running, alone, out on the floor of the valley. He and his wife and Dark and Sim were safe in the mouth of their tunnel.

"He'll never make it," said father. "Do not watch him, woman. It's not a good thing to watch."

They turned away. All except Sim, whose eyes had caught a glint of metal far away. His heart hammered in him, and his eyes blurred. Far away, atop a low mountain, one of those metal seeds from space reflected a dazzling ripple of light! It was like one of his intra-embryo dreams fulfilled! A metal space seed, intact, undamaged, lying on a mountain! There was his future! There was his hope for survival! There was where he would go in a few days, when he was—strange thought—a grown man!

The sun plunged into the valley like molten lava.

The little running child screamed, the sun burned, and the screaming stopped.

Sim's mother walked painfully, with sudden age, down the tunnel, paused, reached up, broke off two last icicles that had formed during the night. She handed one to her husband, kept the other. "We will drink one last toast. To you, to the children."

"To *you*," he nodded to her. "To the children." They lifted the icicles. The warmth melted the ice down into their thirsty mouths.

III

All day the sun seemed to blaze and erupt into the valley. Sim could not see it, but the vivid pictorials in his parents' minds were sufficient evidence of the nature of the day fire. The light ran like mercury, sizzling and roasting the caves, poking inward, but never penetrating deeply enough. It lighted the caves. It made the hollows; of the cliff comfortably warm.

Sim fought to keep his parents young. But no matter how hard he fought with mind and image, they became like mummies before him. His father seemed to dissolve from one stage of oldness to another. This is what will happen to me soon, thought Sim in terror.

Sim grew upon himself. He felt the digestive-eliminatory movements of his body. He was fed every minute, he was continually swallowing, feeding. He began to fit words to images and processes. Such a word was love. It was not an abstraction, but a process, a stir of breath, a smell of morning air, a flutter of heart, the curve of arm holding him, the look in the suspended face of his mother. He saw the processes, then searched behind her suspended face and there was the word, in her brain, ready to use. His throat prepared to speak. Life was pushing him, rushing him along toward oblivion.

He sensed the expansion of his fingernails, the adjustments of his cells; the profusion of his hair, the multiplication of his bones and sinew, the grooving of the soft pale wax of his brain. His brain at birth as clear as a circle of ice, innocent, unmarked, was, an instant later, as if hit with a thrown rock, cracked and marked and patterned in a million crevices of thought and discovery.

His sister, Dark, ran in and out with other little hothouse children, forever eating. His mother trembled over him, not eating, she had no appetite, her eyes were webbed shut.

"Sunset," said his father, at last.

The day was over. The light faded, a wind sounded.

His mother arose. "I want to see the outside world once more . . . just once more. . . ." She stared blindly, shivering.

His father's eyes were shut, he lay against the wall.

"I cannot rise," he whispered faintly. "I cannot."

"Dark!" The mother croaked, the girl came running.

"Here," and Sim was handed to the girl. "Hold to Sim, Dark, feed him, care for him." She gave Sim one last fondling touch.

Dark said not a word, holding Sim, her great green eyes shining wetly.

"Go now," said the mother. "Take him out into the sunset time. Enjoy yourselves. Pick foods, eat. Play."

Dark walked away without looking back. Sim twisted in her grasp, looking over her shoulder with unbelieving, tragic eyes. He cried out and somehow summoned from his lips the first word of his existence:

"Why . . . ?"

He saw his mother stiffen. "The child spoke!"

"Aye," said his father. "Did you hear what he said?"

"I heard," said the mother quietly.

The last thing Sim saw of his living parents was his mother weakly, swayingly, slowly moving across the floor to lie beside her silent husband. That was the last time he ever saw them move.

IV

The night came and passed and then started the second day.

The bodies of all those who had died during the night

were carried in a funeral procession to the top of a small hill. The procession was long, the bodies numerous.

Dark walked in the procession, holding the newly walking Sim by one hand. Only an hour before dawn Sim had learned to walk.

At the top of the hill, Sim saw once again the far off metal seed. Nobody ever looked at it, or spoke of it. Why? Was there some reason? Was it a mirage? Why did they not run toward it? Worship it? Try to get to it and fly away into space?

The funeral words were spoken. The bodies were placed upon the ground where the sun, in a few minutes, would cremate them.

The procession then turned and ran down the hill, eager to have their few minutes of free time running and playing and laughing in the sweet air.

Dark and Sim, chattering like birds, feeding among the rocks, exchanged what they knew of life. He was in his second day, she in her third. They were driven, as always, by the mercurial speed of their lives.

Another piece of his life opened wide.

Fifty young men ran down from the cliffs, holding sharp stones and rock daggers in their thick hands. Shouting, they ran off toward distant black, low lines of small rock cliffs.

"War!"

The thought stood in Sim's brain. It shocked and beat at him. These men were running to fight, to kill, over there in those small black cliffs where other people lived.

But why? Wasn't life short enough without fighting, killing?

From a great distance he heard the sound of conflict, and it made his stomach cold. "Why, Dark, why?"

Dark didn't know. Perhaps they would understand tomorrow. Now, there was the business of eating to sustain and support their lives. Watching Dark was like seeing a lizard forever flicking its pink tongue, forever hungry.

Pale children ran on all sides of them. One beetlelike boy scuttled up the rocks, knocking Sim aside, to take from him a particularly luscious red berry he had found growing under an outcrop.

The child ate hastily of the fruit before Sim could gain his feet. Then Sim hurled himself unsteadily, the two of them fell in a ridiculous jumble, rolling, until Dark pried them, squalling, apart.

Sim bled. A part of him stood off, like a god, and said, "This should not be. Children should not be this way. It is wrong!"

Dark slapped the little intruding boy away. "Get on!" she cried. "What's your name, bad one?"

"Chion!" laughed the boy. "Chion, Chion, Chion!"

Sim glared at him with all the ferocity in his small, unskilled features. He choked. This was his enemy. It was as if he'd waited for an enemy of person as well as scene. He had already understood the avalanches, the heat, the cold, the shortness of life, but these were things of places, of scene—mute, extravagant manifestations of unthinking nature, not motivated save by gravity and radiation. Here, now, in this stridulant Chion he recognized a thinking enemy!

Chion darted off, turned at a distance, taunting:

"Tomorrow I will be big enough to kill you!"

And he vanished around a rock.

More children ran, giggling, by Sim. Which of them would be friends, enemies? How could friends and enemies come about in this impossible, quick lifetime? There was no time to make either, was there?

Dark, knowing his thoughts, drew him away. As they searched for food, she whispered fiercely in his ear. "Enemies are made over things like stolen foods; gifts of long grasses make friends. Enemies come, too, from opinions and thoughts. In five seconds you've made an enemy for life. Life's so short enemies must be made quickly." And she laughed with an irony strange for one so young, who was growing older before her rightful time. "You must fight to protect yourself. Others, superstitious ones, will try killing you. There is a belief, a ridiculous belief, that if one kills another, the murderer partakes of the life energy of the slain, and therefore will live an extra day. You see? As long as that is believed, you're in danger."

But Sim was not listening. Bursting from a flock of delicate girls who tomorrow would be tall, quieter, and who day after that would become shapely and the next day take husbands, Sim caught sight of one small girl whose hair was a violet-blue flame.

She ran past, brushed Sim, their bodies touched. Her eyes, white as silver coins, shone at him. He knew then that he'd found a friend, a love, a wife, one who would a week from now lie with him atop the funeral pyre as sunlight undressed their flesh from bone.

Only the glance, but it held them in mid-motion, one instant.

"Your name?" he shouted after her.

"Lyte!" she called laughingly back.

"I'm Sim," he answered, confused and bewildered.

"Sim!" she repeated it, flashing on. "I'll remember!"

Dark nudged his ribs. "Here, *eat*," she said to the distracted boy. "Eat or you'll never get big enough to catch her."

From nowhere, Chion appeared, running by. "Lyte!" he mocked, dancing malevolently along and away. "Lyte! I'll remember Lyte, too!"

Dark stood tall and reed slender, shaking her dark ebony clouds of hair, sadly. "I see your life before you, little Sim. You'll need weapons soon to fight for this Lyte one. Now, hurry—the sun's coming!"

They ran back to the caves.

V

One-fourth of his life was over! Babyhood was gone. He was now a young boy! Wild rains lashed the valley at nightfall. He watched new river channels cut in the valley, out past the mountain of the metal seed. He stored the knowledge for later use. Each night there was a new river, a bed newly cut.

"What's beyond the valley?" wondered Sim.

"No one's ever been beyond it," explained Dark. "All who tried to reach the plain were frozen to death or burnt. The only land we know's within half an hour's run. Half an hour out and half an hour back."

"No one has ever reached the metal seed, then?"

Dark scoffed. "The Scientists, they try. Silly fools. They don't know enough to stop. It's no use. It's too far."

The Scientists. The word stirred him. He had almost forgotten the vision he had in the moments before and after birth. His voice was eager. "Where are the Scientists?"

Dark looked away from him, "I wouldn't tell you if I knew. They'd kill you, experimenting! I don't want you joining them! Live your life, don't cut it in half trying to reach that silly metal thing on the mountain."

"I'll find out where they are from someone else, then!"

"No one'll tell you! They hate the Scientists. You'll have to find them on your own. And then what? Will you save us? Yes, save us, little boy!" Her face was sullen; already half her life was gone.

"We can't just sit and talk and eat," he protested. "And *nothing* else." He leapt up.

"Go find them!" she retorted acidly. "They'll help you forget. Yes, yes," she spat it out. "Forget your life's over in just a few more days!"

Sim ran through the tunnels, seeking. Sometimes he half imagined where the Scientists were. But then a flood of angry thought from those around him, when he asked the direction to the Scientists' cave, washed over him in confusion and resentment. After all, it was the Scientists' fault that they had been placed upon this terrible world! Sim flinched under the bombardment of oaths and curses.

Quietly he took his seat in a central chamber with the children to listen to the grown men talk. This was the time of education, the Time of Talking. No matter how he chafed at delay, or how great his impatience, even though life slipped fast from him and death approached like a black meteor, he knew his mind needed knowledge. Tonight, then, was the night of school. But he sat uneasily. Only *five* more days of life.

Chion sat across from Sim, his thin-mouthed face arrogant.

Lyte appeared between the two. The last few hours had made her firmer footed, gentler, taller. Her hair shone brighter. She smiled as she sat beside Sim, ignoring Chion. And Chion became rigid at this and ceased eating.

The dialogue crackled, filled the room. Swift as heartbeats, one thousand, two thousand words a minute. Sim learned, his head filled. He did not shut his eyes, but lapsed into a kind of dreaming that was almost intra-embryonic in lassitude and drowsy vividness. In the faint background the words were spoken, and they wove a tapestry of knowledge in his head.

He dreamed of green meadows free of stones, all grass, round and rolling and rushing easily toward a dawn with no taint of freezing, merciless cold or smell of boiled rock or scorched monument. He walked across the green meadow. Overhead the metal seeds flew by in a heaven that was a steady, even temperature. Things were slow, slow, slow.

Birds lingered upon gigantic trees that took a hundred, two hundred, five thousand days to grow. Everything remained in its place, the birds did not flicker nervously at a hint of sun, nor did the trees suck back frightenedly when a ray of sunlight poured over them.

In this dream people strolled, they rarely ran, the heart rhythm of them was evenly languid, not jerking and insane. The grass remained, and did not burn away in torches. The dream people talked always of tomorrow and living and not tomorrow and dying. It all seemed so familiar that when Sim felt someone take his hand he thought it simply another part of the dream.

Lyte's hand lay inside his own. "Dreaming?" she asked.

"Yes."

"Things are balanced. Our minds, to even things, to

balance the unfairness of our living, go back in on ourselves, to find what there is that is good to see."

He beat his hand against the stone floor again and again. "It does not make things fair! I hate it! It reminds me that there is something better, something I have missed! Why can't we be ignorant? Why can't we live and die without knowing that this is an abnormal living?" And his breath rushed harshly from his half-open, constricted mouth.

"There is purpose in everything," said Lyte. "This gives us purpose, makes us work, plan, try to find a way."

His eyes were hot emeralds in his face. "I walked up a hill of grass, very slowly," he said.

"The same hill of grass I walked an hour ago?" asked Lyte.

"Perhaps. Close enough to it. The dream is better than the reality." He flexed his eyes, narrowed them. "I watched people and they did not eat."

"Or talk?"

"Or talk, either. And we always are eating, always talking. Sometimes those people in the dream sprawled with their eyes shut, not moving a muscle."

As Lyte stared down into his face a terrible thing happened. He imagined her face blackening, wrinkling, twisting into knots of agedness. The hair blew out like

284

snow about her ears, the eyes were like discolored coins caught in a web of lashes. Her teeth sank away from her lips, the delicate fingers hung like charred twigs from her atrophied wrists. Her beauty was consumed and wasted even as he watched, and when he seized her, in terror, he cried out, for he imagined his own hand corroded, and he choked back a cry.

"Sim, what's wrong?"

The saliva in his mouth dried at the taste of the words.

"Five more days . . ."

"The Scientists."

Sim started. Who'd spoken? In the dim light a tall man talked. "The Scientists crashed us on this world, and now have wasted thousands of lives and time. It's no use. It's no use. Tolerate them but give them none of your time. You only live once, remember."

Where were these hated Scientists? Now, after the Learning, the Time of Talking, he was ready to find them. Now, at least, he knew enough to begin his fight for freedom, for the ship!

"Sim, where're you going?"

But Sim was gone. The echo of his running feet died away down a shaft of polished stone.

* * *

It seemed that half the night was wasted. He blundered into a dozen dead ends. Many times he was attacked by the insane young men who wanted his life energy. Their superstitious ravings echoed after him. The gashes of their hungry fingernails covered his body.

He found what he looked for.

A half dozen men gathered in a small basalt cave deep down in the cliff lode. On a table before them lay objects which, though unfamiliar, struck harmonious chords in Sim.

The Scientists worked in sets, old men doing important work, young men learning, asking questions; and at their feet were three small children. They were a process. Every eight days there was an entirely new set of scientists working on any one problem. The amount of work done was terribly inadequate. They grew old, fell dead just when they were beginning their creative period. The creative time of any one individual was perhaps a matter of twelve hours out of his entire span. Three quarters of one's life was spent learning, a brief interval of creative power, then senility, insanity, death.

The men turned as Sim entered.

"Don't tell me we have a recruit?" said the eldest of them.

"I don't believe it," said another, younger one. "Chase

him away. He's probably one of those warmongers."

"No, no," objected the elder one, moving with little shuffles of his bare feet toward Sim. "Come in, come in, boy." He had friendly eyes, slow eyes, unlike those of the swift inhabitants of the upper caves. Gray and quiet. "What do you want?"

Sim hesitated, lowered his head, unable to meet the quiet, gentle gaze. "I want to live," he whispered.

The old man laughed quietly. He touched Sim's shoulder. "Are you a new breed? Are you sick?" he queried of Sim, half seriously. "Why aren't you playing? Why aren't you readying yourself for the time of love and marriage and children? Don't you know that tomorrow night you'll be almost grown? Don't you realize that if you are not careful you'll miss all of life?" He stopped.

Sim moved his eyes back and forth with each query. He blinked at the instruments on the table top. "Shouldn't I be here?" he asked.

"Certainly," roared the old man, sternly. "But it's a miracle you are. We've had no volunteers from the rank and file for a thousand days! We've had to breed our own scientists, a closed unit! Count us! Six! Six men! And three children! Are we not overwhelming?" The old man spat upon the stone floor. "We ask for volunteers and the people shout back at us, 'Get someone else!' or 'We have no time!' And you know why they say that?"

"No." Sim flinched.

"Because they're selfish. They'd like to live longer, yes, but they know that anything they do cannot possibly insure their *own* lives any extra time. It might guarantee longer life to some future offspring of theirs. But they won't give up their love, their brief youth, give up one interval of sunset or sunrise!"

Sim leaned against the table, earnestly. "I understand."

"You do?" The old man stared at him blindly. He sighed and slapped the child's arm gently. "Yes, of course, you do. It's too much to expect anyone to understand, anymore. You're rare."

The others moved in around Sim and the old man.

"I am Dienc. Tomorrow night Cort here will be in my place. I'll be dead by then. And the night after that someone else will be in Cort's place, and then you, if you work and believe—but first, I give you a chance. Return to your playmates if you want. There is someone you love? Return to her. Life is short. Why should you care for the unborn to come? You have a right to youth. Go now, if you want. Because if you stay you'll have no time for anything but working and growing old and dying at your work. But it is good work. Well?"

Sim looked at the tunnel. From a distance the wind roared and blew, the smells of cooking and the patter of naked feet sounded, and the laughter of young people was an increasingly good thing to hear. He shook his head, impatiently, and his eyes were wet.

"I will stay," he said.

VI

The third night and third day passed. It was the fourth night. Sim was drawn into their living. He learned about that metal seed upon the top of the far mountain. He heard of the original seeds—things called "ships" that crashed and how the survivors hid and dug in the cliffs, grew old swiftly and in their scrabbling to barely survive, forgot all science. Knowledge of mechanical things had no chance of survival in such a volcanic civilization. There was only NOW for each human.

Yesterday didn't matter, tomorrow stared them vividly in their very faces. But somehow the radiations that had forced their aging had also induced a kind of telepathic communication whereby philosophies and impressions were absorbed by the newborn. Racial memory, growing instinctively, preserved memories of another time.

"Why don't we go to that ship on the mountain?" asked Sim.

"It is too far. We would need protection from the sun," explained Dienc.

"Have you tried to make protection?"

"Salves and ointments, suits of stone and bird-wing and, recently, crude metals. None of which worked. In ten thousand more lifetimes perhaps we'll have made a metal in which will flow cool water to protect us on the march to the ship. But we work so slowly, so blindly. This morning, mature, I took up my instruments. Tomorrow, dying, I lay them down. What can one man do in one day? If we had ten thousand men, the problem would be solved. . . ."

"I will go to the ship," said Sim.

"Then you will die," said the old man. A silence had fallen on the room at Sim's words. Then the men stared at Sim. "You are a very selfish boy."

"Selfish!" cried Sim, resentfully.

The old man patted the air. "Selfish in a way I like. You want to live longer, you'll do anything for that. You will try for the ship. But I tell you it is useless. Yet, if you want to, I cannot stop you. At least you will not be like those among us who go to war for an extra few days of life."

"War?" asked Sim. "How can there be war here?"

And a shudder ran through him. He did not understand.

"Tomorrow will be time enough for that," said Dienc. "Listen to me, now."

The night passed.

VII

It was morning. Lyte came shouting and sobbing down a corridor, and ran full into his arms. She had changed again. She was older, again, more beautiful. She was shaking and she held to him. "Sim, they're coming after you!"

Bare feet marched down the corridor, surged inward at the opening. Chion stood grinning there, taller, too, a sharp rock in either of his hands. "Oh, there you are, Sim!"

"Go away!" cried Lyte, savagely whirling on him.

"Not until we take Sim with us," Chion assured her. Then, smiling at Sim. "*If*, that is, he is with us in the fight."

Dienc shuffled forward, his eye weakly fluttering, his bird-like hands fumbling in the air. "Leave!" he shrilled angrily. "This boy is a Scientist now. He works with us."

Chion ceased smiling. "There is better work to be done. We go now to fight the people in the farthest cliffs." His eyes glittered anxiously. "Of course, you will come with us, Sim?"

"No, no!" Lyte clutched at his arm.

Sim patted her shoulder, then turned to Chion. "Why are you attacking these people?"

"There are three extra days for those who go with us to fight."

"Three extra days! Of living?"

Chion nodded firmly. "If we win, we live eleven days instead of eight. The cliffs they live in, something about the mineral in it that protects you from radiation! Think of it, Sim, three long, good days of life. Will you join us?"

Dienc interrupted. "Get along without him. Sim is my pupil!"

Chion snorted. "Go die, old man. By sunset tonight you'll be charred bone. Who are you to order us? We are young, we want to live longer."

Eleven days. The words were unbelievable to Sim. Eleven days. Now he understood why there was war. Who wouldn't fight to have his life lengthened by almost half its total. So many more days of living! Yes. Why not, indeed!

"Three extra days," called Dienc, stridently, "*if* you live to enjoy them. If you're not killed in battle. *If. If!* You have never won yet. You have always lost!"

"But this time," Chion declared sharply, "we'll win!"

Sim was bewildered. "But we are all of the same ancestors. Why don't we all share the best cliffs?"

Chion laughed and adjusted a sharp stone in his hand. "Those who live in the best cliffs think they are better than us. That is always man's attitude when he has power. The cliffs there, besides, are smaller, there's room for only three hundred people in them."

Three extra days.

"I'll go with you," Sim said to Chion.

"Fine!" Chion was very glad, much too glad at the decision.

Dienc gasped.

Sim turned to Dienc and Lyte. "If I fight, and win, I will be half a mile closer to the ship. And I'll have three extra days in which to strive to reach the ship. That seems the only thing for me to do."

Dienc nodded, sadly. "It *is* the only thing. I believe you. Go along now."

"Good-bye," said Sim.

The old man looked surprised, then he laughed as at a little joke on himself. "That's right—I won't see you again, will I? Good-bye, then." And they shook hands.

They went out, Chion, Sim, and Lyte, together, followed by the others, all children growing swiftly into fighting men. And the light in Chion's eyes was not a good thing to see.

*   *   *

Lyte went with him. She chose his rocks for him and carried them. She would not go back, no matter how he pleaded. The sun was just beyond the horizon and they marched across the valley.

"Please, Lyte, go back!"

"And wait for Chion to return?" she said. "He plans that when you die I will be his mate." She shook out her unbelievable blue-white curls of hair defiantly. "But I'll be with you. If you fall, I fall."

Sim's face hardened. He was tall. The world had shrunk during the night. Children packs screamed by hilarious in their food-searching and he looked at them with alien wonder: could it be only four days ago he'd been like these? Strange. There was a sense of many days in his mind, as if he'd really lived a thousand days. There was a dimension of incident and thought so thick, so multicolored, so richly diverse in his head that it was not to be believed so much could happen in so short a time.

The fighting men ran in clusters of two or three. Sim looked ahead at the rising line of small ebon cliffs. This, then, he said to himself, is my fourth day. And still I am no closer to the ship, or to anything, not even—he heard the light tread of Lyte beside him—not even to her who bears my weapons and picks me ripe berries.

One-half of his life was gone. Or a third of it—If he won this battle. *If.*

He ran easily, lifting, letting fall his legs. This is the day of my physical awareness, as I run I feed, as I feed I grow and as I grow I turn eyes to Lyte with a kind of dizzying vertigo. And she looks upon me with the same gentleness of thought. This is the day of our youth. Are we wasting it? Are we losing it on a dream, a folly?

Distantly he heard laughter. As a child he'd questioned it. Now he understood laughter. This particular laughter was made of climbing high rocks and plucking the greenest blades and drinking the headiest vintage from the morning ices and eating of the rock-fruits and tasting of young lips in new appetite.

They neared the cliffs of the enemy.

He saw the slender erectness of Lyte. The new surprise of her neck where if you touched you could time her pulse; the fingers which cupped in your own were animate and supple and never still; the . . .

Lyte snapped her head to one side. "Look ahead!" she cried. "See what is to come—look only ahead."

He felt that they were racing by part of their lives, leaving their youth on the pathside, without so much as a glance.

"I am blind with looking at stones," he said, running.

"Find new stones, then!"

"I see stones—" His voice grew gentle as the palm of her hand. The landscape floated under him. Everything was like a fine wind, blowing dreamily. "I see stones that make a ravine that lies in a cool shadow where the stone-berries are thick as tears. You touch a boulder and the berries fall in silent red avalanches, and the grass is very tender . . ."

"I do not see it!" She increased her pace, turning her head away.

He saw the floss upon her neck, like the small moss that grows silvery and light on the cool side of pebbles, that stirs if you breathe the lightest breath upon it. He looked upon himself, his hands clenched as he heaved himself forward toward death. Already his hands were veined and youth-swollen.

Lyte handed him food to eat.

"I am not hungry," he said.

"Eat, keep your mouth full," she commanded sharply, "so you will be strong for battle."

"Gods!" He roared, anguished. "Who cares for battles!"

Ahead of them, rocks hailed down, thudding. A man fell with his skull split wide. The war was begun.

Lyte passed the weapons to him. They ran without

another word until they entered the killing ground.

The boulders began to roll in a synthetic avalanche from the battlements of the enemy!

Only one thought was in his mind now. To kill, to lessen the life of someone else so he could live, to gain a foothold here and live long enough to make a stab at the ship. He ducked, he weaved, he clutched stones and hurled them up. His left hand held a flat stone shield with which he diverted the swiftly plummeting rocks. There was a spatting sound everywhere. Lyte ran with him, encouraging him. Two men dropped before him, slain, their breasts cleaved to the bone, their blood springing out in unbelievable founts.

It was a useless conflict. Sim realized instantly how insane the venture was. They could never storm the cliff. A solid wall of rocks rained down. A dozen men dropped with shards of ebony in their brains, a half dozen more showed drooping, broken arms. One screamed and the upthrust white joint of his knee was exposed as the flesh was pulled away by two successive blows of well-aimed granite. Men stumbled over one another.

The muscles in his cheeks pulled tight and he began to wonder why he had ever come. But his raised eyes, as he danced from side to side, weaving and bobbing, sought always the cliffs. He wanted to live there so intensely, to have his chance. He would have to stick it out. But the heart was gone from him.

Lyte screamed piercingly. Sim, his heart panicking, twisted and saw that her hand was loose at the wrist, with an ugly wound bleeding profusely on the back of the knuckles. She clamped it under her armpit to soothe the pain. The anger rose in him and exploded. In his fury he raced forward, throwing his missiles with deadly accuracy. He saw a man topple and flail down, falling from one level to another of the caves, a victim of his shot. He must have been screaming, for his lungs were bursting open and closed and his throat was raw, and the ground spun madly under his racing feet.

The stone that clipped his head sent him reeling and plunging back. He ate sand. The universe dissolved into purple whorls. He could not get up. He lay and knew that this was his last day, his last time. The battle raged around him, dimly he felt Lyte over him. Her hands cooled his head, she tried to drag him out of range, but he lay gasping and telling her to leave him.

"Stop!" shouted a voice. The whole war seemed to give pause. "Retreat!" commanded the voice swiftly. And as Sim watched, lying upon his side, his comrades turned and fled back toward home.

"The sun is coming, our time is up!" He saw their muscled backs, their moving, tensing, flickering legs go up and down. The dead were left upon the field. The wounded cried for help. But there was no time for the wounded. There was only time for swift men to run the gauntlet home and, their lungs aching and raw with heated air, burst into their tunnels before the sun burnt and killed them.

The sun!

Sim saw another figure racing toward him. It was Chion! Lyte was helping Sim to his feet, whispering helpfully to him. "Can you walk?" she asked. And he groaned and said, "I think so." "Walk then," she said. "Walk slowly, and then faster and faster. We'll make it, I know we will."

Sim got to his feet, stood swaying. Chion raced up, a strange expression cutting lines in his cheeks, his eyes shining with battle. Pushing Lyte abruptly aside he seized upon a rock and dealt Sim a jolting blow upon his ankle that laid wide the flesh. All of this was done quite silently.

Now he stood back, still not speaking, grinning like an animal from the night mountains, his chest panting in and out, looking from the thing he had done, to Lyte, and back. He got his breath. "He'll never make it," he nodded at Sim. "We'll have to leave him here. Come along, Lyte."

Lyte, like a cat-animal, sprang upon Chion, searching for his eyes, shrieking through her exposed, hard-pressed teeth. Her fingers stroked great bloody furrows down Chion's arms and again, instantly, down his neck. Chion, with an oath, sprang away from her. She hurled a rock at him. Grunting, he let it miss him, then ran off a few yards. "Fool!" he cried, turning to scorn her. "Come along with me. Sim will be dead in a few minutes. Come along!"

Lyte turned her back on him. "I will go if you carry me."

Chion's face changed. His eyes lost their gleaming. "There is no time. We would both die if I carried you."

Lyte looked through and beyond him. "Carry me, then, for that's how I wish it to be."

Without another word, glancing fearfully at the sun, Chion fled. His footsteps sped away and vanished from hearing. "May he fall and break his neck," whispered Lyte, savagely glaring at his form as it skirted a ravine. She returned to Sim. "Can you walk?"

Agonies of pain shot up his leg from the wounded ankle. He nodded ironically. "We could make it to the cave in two hours, walking. I have an idea, Lyte. Carry me." And he smiled with the grim joke.

She took his arm. "Nevertheless we'll walk. Come."

"No," he said. "We're staying here."

"But why?"

"We came to seek a home here. If we walk we will die. I would rather die here. How much time have we?"

Together they measured the sun. "A few minutes," she said, her voice flat and dull. She held close to him.

The black rocks of the cliff were paling into deep purples and browns as the sun began to flood the world.

What a fool he was! He should have stayed and worked with Dienc, and thought and dreamed.

With the sinews of his neck standing out defiantly he bellowed upward at the cliff holes.

"Send me down one man to do battle!"

Silence. His voice echoed from the cliff. The air was warm.

"It's no use," said Lyte, "They'll pay no attention."

He shouted again. "Hear me!" He stood with his weight on his good foot, his injured left leg throbbing and pulsating with pain. He shook a fist. "Send down a warrior who is no coward! I will not turn and run home! I have come to fight a fair fight! Send a man who will fight for the right to his cave! Him I will surely kill!"

More silence. A wave of heat passed over the land, receded.

"Oh, surely," mocked Sim, hands on naked hips, head

back, mouth wide, "surely there's one among you not afraid to fight a cripple!" Silence. "No?" Silence.

"Then I have miscalculated you. I'm wrong. I'll stand here, then, until the sun shucks the flesh off my bone in black scraps, and call you the filthy names you deserve."

He got an answer.

"I do not like being called names," replied a man's voice.

Sim leaned forward, forgetting his crippled foot.

A huge man appeared in a cave mouth on the third level.

"Come down," urged Sim. "Come down, fat one, and kill me."

The man scowled seriously at his opponent a moment, then lumbered slowly down the path, his hands empty of any weapons. Immediately every cave above clustered with heads. An audience for this drama.

The man approached Sim. "We will fight by the rules, if you know them."

"I'll learn as we go," replied Sim.

This pleased the man and he looked at Sim warily, but not unkindly. "This much I will tell you," offered the man generously. "If you die, I will give your mate shelter and she will live as she pleases, because she is the wife of a good man."

Sim nodded swiftly. "I am ready," he said.

"The rules are simple. We do not touch each other, save with stones. The stones and the sun will do either of us in. Now is the time—"

VIII

A tip of the sun showed on the horizon. "My name is Nhoj," said Sim's enemy, casually taking up a handful of pebbles and stones, weighing them. Sim did likewise. He was hungry. He had not eaten for many minutes. Hunger was the curse of this planet's peoples—a perpetual demanding of empty stomachs for more, more food. His blood flushed weakly, shot tinglingly through veins in jolting throbs of heat and pressure, his rib cage shoved out, went in, shoved out again, impatiently.

"Now!" roared the three hundred watchers from the cliffs. "Now!" they clamored, the men and women and children balanced, in turmoil on the ledges. "Now! Begin!"

As if at a cue, the sun arose. It smote them a blow as with a flat, sizzling stone. The two men staggered under the molten impact, sweat broke from their naked thighs and loins, under their arms and on their faces was a glaze like fine glass.

Nhoj shifted his huge weight and looked at the sun as if in no hurry to fight. Then, silently, with no warning, he snapped out a pebble with a startling trigger-flick of thumb and forefinger. It caught Sim flat on the cheek, staggered him back, so that a rocket of unbearable pain climbed up his crippled foot and burst into nervous explosion at the pit of his stomach. He tasted blood from his bleeding cheek.

Nhoj moved serenely. Three more flicks of his magical hands and three tiny, seemingly harmless bits of stone flew like whistling birds. Each of them found a target, slammed it. The nerve centers of Sim's body! One hit his stomach so that ten hours' eating almost slid up his throat. A second got his forehead, a third his neck. He collapsed to the boiling sand. His knee made a wrenching sound on the hard earth. His face was colorless and his eyes, squeezed tight, were pushing tears out from the hot, quivering lids. But even as he had fallen he had let loose, with wild force, his handful of stones!

The stones purred in the air. One of them, and only one, struck Nhoj. Upon the left eyeball. Nhoj moaned and laid his hands in the next instant to his shattered eye.

Sim choked out a bitter, sighing laugh. This much triumph he had. The eye of his opponent. It would give him . . . Time. Oh, gods, he thought, his stomach retching sickly, fighting for breath, this is a world of time. Give me a little more, just a trifle!

Nhoj, one-eyed, weaving with pain, pelted the writhing body of Sim, but his aim was off now, the stones flew to one side or if they struck at all they were weak and spent and lifeless.

Sim forced himself half erect. From the corners of his eyes he saw Lyte, waiting, staring at him, her lips breathing words of encouragement and hope. He was bathed in sweat, as if a rain spray had showered him down.

The sun was now fully over the horizon. You could smell it. Stones glinted like mirrors, the sand began to roil and bubble. Illusions sprang up everywhere in the valley. Instead of one warrior Nhoj he was confronted by a dozen, each in an upright position, preparing to launch another missile. A dozen irregular warriors who shimmered in the golden menace of day, like bronze gongs smitten, quivered in one vision!

Sim was breathing desperately. His nostrils flared and sucked and his mouth drank thirstily of flame instead of oxygen. His lungs took fire like silk torches and his body was consumed. The sweat spilled from his pores to be instantly evaporated. He felt himself shriveling, shriveling in on himself, he imagined himself looking like his father, old, sunken, slight, withered! Where was the sand? Could he move? Yes. The world wriggled under him, but now he was on his feet.

There would be no more fighting.

A murmur from the cliff told this. The sunburnt faces of the high audience gaped and jeered and shouted encouragement to their warrior. "Stand straight, Nhoj, save your strength now! Stand tall and perspire!" they urged him. And Nhoj stood, swaying lightly, swaying slowly, a pendulum in an incandescent fiery breath from the skyline. "Don't move, Nhoj, save your heart, save your power!"

"The Test, The Test!" said the people on the heights. "The test of the sun."

And this was the worst part of the fight. Sim squinted painfully at the distorted illusion of cliff. He thought he saw his parents; father with his defeated face, his green eyes burning, mother with her hair blowing like a cloud of gray smoke in the fire wind. He must get up to them, live for and with them!

Behind him, Sim heard Lyte whimper softly. There was a whisper of flesh against sand. She had fallen. He did not dare turn. The strength of turning would bring him thundering down in pain and darkness.

His knees bent. If I fall, he thought, I'll lie here and become ashes. Where was Nhoj? Nhoj was there, a few yards from him, standing bent, slick with perspiration, looking as if he were being hit over the spine with great hammers of destruction.

"Fall, Nhoj! Fall!" thought Sim. "Fall, fall! Fall so I can take your place!"

But Nhoj did not fall. One by one the pebbles in his half-loose left hand plummeted to the broiling sands and Nhoj's lips peeled back, the saliva burned away from his lips and his eyes glazed. But he did not fall. The will to live was strong in him. He hung as if by a wire.

Sim fell to one knee!

"Ahh!" wailed the knowing voices from the cliff. They were watching death. Sim jerked his head up, smiling mechanically, foolishly as if caught in the act of doing something silly. "No, no," he insisted drowsily, and got back up again. There was so much pain he was all one ringing numbness. A whirring, buzzing, frying sound filled the land. High up, an avalanche came down like a curtain on a drama, making no noise. Everything was quiet except for a steady humming. He saw fifty images of Nhoj now, dressed in armors of sweat, eyes puffed with torture, cheeks sunken, lips peeled back like the rind of a drying fruit. But the wire still held him.

"Now," muttered Sim, sluggishly, with a thick, baked

tongue between his blazing teeth. "Now I'll fall and lie and dream." He said it with slow, thoughtful pleasure. He planned it. He knew how it must be done. He would do it accurately. He lifted his head to see if the audience was watching.

They were gone!

The sun had driven them back in. All save one or two brave ones. Sim laughed drunkenly and watched the sweat gather on his dead hands, hesitate, drop off, plunge down toward sand and turn to steam halfway there.

Nhoj fell.

The wire was cut. Nhoj fell flat upon his stomach, a gout of blood kicked from his mouth. His eyes rolled back into a white, senseless insanity.

Nhoj fell. So did his fifty duplicate illusions.

All across the valley the winds sang and moaned and Sim saw a blue lake with a blue river feeding it and low white houses near the river with people going and coming in the houses and among the tall green trees. Trees taller than seven men, beside the river mirage.

"Now," explained Sim to himself at last, "Now I can fall. Right—into—that—lake."

He fell forward.

He was shocked when he felt the hands eagerly stop him

in mid-plunge, lift him, hurry him off, high in the hungry air, like a torch held and waved, ablaze.

"How strange is death," he thought, and blackness took him.

He wakened to the flow of cool water on his cheeks.

He opened his eyes fearfully. Lyte held his head upon her lap, her fingers were moving food to his mouth. He was tremendously hungry and tired, but fear squeezed both of these things away. He struggled upward, seeing the strange cave contours overhead.

"What time is it?" he demanded.

"The same day as the contest. Be quiet," she said.

"The same day!"

She nodded amusedly. "You've lost nothing of your life. This is Nhoj's cave. We are inside the black cliff. We will live three extra days. Satisfied? Lie down."

"Nhoj is dead?" He fell back, panting, his heart slamming his ribs. He relaxed slowly. "I won. I won," he breathed.

"Nhoj is dead. So were we, almost. They carried us in from outside only in time."

He ate ravenously. "We have no time to waste. We must get strong. My leg—" He looked at it, tested it. There was a swath of long yellow grasses around it and the ache had died away. Even as he watched, the terrific pulsings of his body went to work and cured away the impurities under the bandages. It *has* to be strong by sunset, he thought. It *has* to be.

He got up and limped around the cave like a captured animal. He felt Lyte's eyes upon him. He could not meet her gaze. Finally, helplessly, he turned.

She interrupted him. "You want to go on to the ship?" she asked, softly. "Tonight? When the sun goes down?"

He took a breath, exhaled it. "Yes."

"You couldn't possibly wait until morning?"

"No!"

"Then I'll go with you."

"No!"

"If I lag behind, let me. There's nothing here for me."

They stared at each other a long while. He shrugged wearily.

"All right," he said, at last. "I couldn't stop you, I know that. We'll go together."

IX

They waited in the mouth of their new cave. The sun set. The stones cooled so that one could walk on them. It was almost time for the leaping out and the running toward the distant, glittering metal seed that lay on the far mountain.

Soon would come the rains. And Sim thought back over all the times he had watched the rains thicken into creeks, into rivers that cut new beds each night. One night there would be a river running north, the next a river running northeast, the third night a river running due west. The valley was continually cut and scarred by the torrents. Earthquakes and avalanches filled the old beds. New ones were the order of the day. It was this idea of the river and the directions of the river that he had turned over in his head for many hours. It might possibly— Well, he would wait and see.

He noticed how living in this new cliff had slowed his pulse, slowed everything. A mineral result, protection against the solar radiations. Life was still swift, but not as swift as before.

"Now, Sim!" cried Lyte.

They ran. Between the hot death and the cold one. Together, away from the cliffs, out toward the distant, beckoning ship.

Never had they run this way in their lives. The sound of their feet running was a hard, insistent clatter over vast oblongs of rock, down into ravines, up the sides, and on again. They raked the air in and out their lungs. Behind them the cliffs faded into things they could never turn back to now.

They did not eat as they ran. They had eaten to the bursting point in the cave, to save time. Now it was only running, a lifting of legs, a balancing of bent elbows, a convulsion of muscles, a slaking in of air that had been fiery and was now cooling.

"Are they watching us?"

Lyte's breathless voice snatched at his ears above the pound of his heart.

Who? But he knew the answer. The cliff peoples, of course. How long had it been since a race like this one? A thousand days? Ten thousand? How long since someone had taken the chance and sprinted with an entire civilization's eyes upon their backs, into gullies, across cooling plain. Were there lovers pausing in their laughter back there, gazing at the two tiny dots that were a man and woman running toward destiny? Were children eating of new fruits and stopping in their play to see the two people racing against time? Was Dienc still living, narrowing hairy eyebrows down over fading eyes, shouting them on in a feeble, rasping voice, shaking a twisted hand? Were there jeers? Were they being called fools, idiots? And in the midst of the name-calling, were people praying them on, hoping they would reach the ship?

Sim took a quick glance at the sky, which was beginning to bruise with the coming night. Out of nowhere clouds materialized and a light shower trailed across a gully two hundred yards ahead of them. Lightning beat upon distant mountains and there was a strong scent of ozone on the disturbed air.

"The halfway mark," panted Sim, and he saw Lyte's face half turn, longingly looking back at the life she was leaving. "Now's the time, if we want to turn back, we still have time. Another minute—"

Thunder snarled in the mountains. An avalanche started out small and ended up huge and monstrous in a deep fissure. Light rain dotted Lyte's smooth white skin. In a minute her hair was glistening and soggy with rain.

"Too late, now," she shouted over the patting rhythm of her own naked feet. "We've got to go ahead!"

And it was too late. Sim knew, judging the distances, that there was no turning back now.

His leg began to pain him. He favored it, slowing. A wind came up swiftly. A cold wind that bit into the skin. But it came from the cliffs behind them, helped rather than hindered them. An omen? he wondered. No.

For as the minutes went by it grew upon him how poorly he had estimated the distance. Their time was dwindling out, but they were still an impossible distance from the ship. He said nothing, but the impotent anger at the slow muscles in his legs welled up into bitterly hot tears in his eyes.

He knew that Lyte was thinking the same as himself. But she flew along like a white bird, seeming hardly to touch ground. He heard her breath go out and in her throat, like a clean, sharp knife in its sheath.

Half the sky was dark. The first stars were peering through lengths of black cloud. Lightning jiggled a path along a rim just ahead of them. A full thunderstorm of violent rain and exploding electricity fell upon them.

They slipped and skidded on moss-smooth pebbles. Lyte fell, scrambled up again with a burning oath. Her body was scarred and dirty. The rain washed over her.

The rain came down and cried on Sim. It filled his eyes and ran in rivers down his spine and he wanted to cry with it.

Lyte fell and did not rise, sucking her breath, her breasts quivering.

He picked her up and held her. "Run, Lyte, please, run!"

"Leave me, Sim. Go ahead!" The rain filled her mouth.

There was water everywhere. "It's no use. Go on without me."

He stood there, cold and powerless, his thoughts sagging, the flame of hope blinking out. All the world was blackness, cold falling sheaths of water, and despair.

"We'll walk, then," he said. "And keep walking, and resting."

They walked for fifty yards, easily, slowly, like children out for a stroll. The gully ahead of them filled with water that went sliding away with a swift wet sound, toward the horizon.

Sim cried out. Tugging at Lyte he raced forward. "A new channel," he said, pointing. "Each day the rain cuts a new channel. Here, Lyte!" He leaned over the floodwaters.

He dived in, taking her with him.

The flood swept them like bits of wood. They fought to stay upright, the water got into their mouths, their noses. The land swept by on both sides of them. Clutching Lyte's fingers with insane strength, Sim felt himself hurled end over end, saw flicks of lightning on high, and a new fierce hope was born in him. They could no longer run—well, then they would let the water do the running for them.

With a speed that dashed them against rocks, split open their shoulders, abraded their legs, the new, brief river carried them. "This way!" Sim shouted over a salvo of thunder and steered frantically toward the opposite side of the gully. The mountain where the ship lay was just ahead. They must not pass it by. They fought in the transporting liquid and were slammed against the far side. Sim leaped up, caught at an overhanging rock, locked Lyte in his legs, and drew himself hand over hand upward.

As quickly as it had come, the storm was gone. The lightning faded. The rain ceased. The clouds melted and fell away over the sky. The wind whispered into silence.

"The ship!" Lyte lay upon the ground. "The ship, Sim. This is the mountain of the ship!"

Now the cold came. The killing cold.

They forced themselves drunkenly up the mountain. The cold slid along their limbs, got into their arteries like a chemical and slowed them.

Ahead of them, with a fresh-washed sheen, lay the ship. It was a dream. Sim could not believe that they were actually so near it. Two hundred yards. One hundred and seventy yards.

The ground became covered with ice. They slipped and fell again and again. Behind them the river was frozen into a blue-white snake of cold solidity. A few last drops of rain from somewhere came down as hard pellets.

Sim fell against the bulk of the ship. He was actually touching it. Touching it! He heard Lyte whimpering in her constricted throat. This was the metal, the ship. How many others had touched it in the long days? He and Lyte had made it!

Then, as cold as the air, his veins were chilled.

Where was the entrance?

You run, you swim, you almost drown, you curse, you sweat, you work, you reach a mountain, you go up it, you hammer on metal, you shout with relief, and then—you can't find the entrance.

He fought to control himself. Slowly, he told himself, but not too slowly, go around the ship. The metal slid under his searching hands, so cold that his hands, sweating, almost froze to it. Now, far around to the side. Lyte moved with him. The cold held them like a fist. It began to squeeze.

The entrance.

Metal. Cold, immutable metal. A thin line of opening at the sealing point. Throwing all caution aside, he beat at it. He felt his stomach seething with cold. His fingers were numb, his eyes were half frozen in their sockets. He began to beat and search and scream against the metal door. "Open up! Open up!" He staggered. He had struck something . . . A *click!*

The air lock sighed. With a whispering of metal on rubber beddings, the door swung softly sidewise and vanished back.

He saw Lyte run forward, clutch at her throat, and drop inside a small shiny chamber. He shuffled after her, blankly.

The air-lock door sealed shut behind him.

He could not breathe. His heart began to slow, to stop.

They were trapped inside the ship now, and something was happening. He sank down to his knees and choked for air.

The ship he had come to for salvation was now slowing his pulse, darkening his brain, poisoning him. With a starved, faint kind of expiring terror, he realized that he was dying.

Blackness.

He had a dim sense of time passing, of thinking, struggling, to make his heart go quick, quick. . . . To make his eyes focus. But the fluid in his body lagged quietly through his settling veins and he heard his pulses thud, pause, thud, pause and thud again with lulling intermissions.

He could not move, not a hand or leg or finger. It was an effort to lift the tonnage of his eyelashes. He could not shift his face even, to see Lyte lying beside him.

From a distance came her irregular breathing. It was like the sound a wounded bird makes with his dry, unraveled pinions. She was so close he could almost feel the heat of her; yet she seemed a long way removed.

I'm getting cold! he thought. Is this death? This slowing of blood, of my heart, this cooling of my body, this drowsy thinking of thoughts?

Staring at the ship's ceiling he traced its intricate system of tubes and machines. The knowledge, the purpose of the ship, its actions, seeped into him. He began to understand in a kind of revealing lassitude just what these things were his eyes rested upon. Slow. Slow.

There was an instrument with a gleaming white dial.

Its purpose?

He drudged away at the problem, like a man under-water.

People had used the dial. Touched it. People had repaired it. Installed it. People had dreamed of it before the building, before the installing, before the repairing and touching and using. The dial contained memory of use and manu-facture, its very shape was a dream-memory telling Sim why and for what it had been built. Given time, looking at anything, he could draw from it the knowledge he desired. Some dim part of him reached out, dissected the contents of things, analyzed them.

This dial measured time!

Millions of hours of time!

But how could that be? Sim's eyes dilated, hot and glittering. Where were humans who needed such an instrument?

Blood thrummed and beat behind his eyes. He closed them.

Panic came to him. The day was passing. I am lying here, he thought, and my life slips away. I cannot move. My youth is passing. How long before I can move?

Through a kind of porthole he saw the night pass, the day come, the day pass, and again another night. Stars danced frostily.

I will lie here for four or five days, wrinkling and withering, he thought. This ship will not let me move. How much better if I had stayed in my home cliff, lived, enjoyed this short life. What good has it done to come here? I'm missing all the twilights and dawns. I'll never touch Lyte, though she's here at my side.

Delirium. His mind floated up. His thoughts whirled through the metal ship. He smelled the razor-sharp smell of joined metal. He heard the hull contract with night, relax with day.

Dawn.

Already—another dawn!

Today I would have been fully grown. His jaw clenched. I must get up. I must move. I must enjoy this time.

But he didn't move. He felt his blood pump sleepily from chamber to red chamber in his heart, on down and around through his dead body, to be purified by his folding and unfolding lungs.

The ship grew warm. From somewhere a machine clicked. Automatically the temperature cooled. A controlled gust of air flushed the room.

Night again. And then another day.

He lay and saw four days of his life pass.

He did not try to fight. It was no use. His life was over.

He didn't want to turn his head now. He didn't want to see Lyte with her face like his tortured mother's—eyelids like gray ash flakes, eyes like beaten, sanded metal, cheeks like eroded stones. He didn't want to see a throat like parched thongs of yellow grass, hands the pattern of smoke risen from a fire, breasts like dessicated rinds and hair stubbly and unshorn as moist gray weeds!

And himself? How did *he* look? Was his jaw sunken, the flesh of his eyes pitted, his brow lined and age-scarred?

His strength began to return. He felt his heart beating so slow that it was amazing. One hundred beats a minute.

Impossible. He felt so cool, so thoughtful, so easy.

His head fell over to one side. He stared at Lyte. He shouted in surprise.

She was young and fair.

She was looking at him, too weak to say anything. Her eyes were like tiny silver medals, her throat curved like the arm of a child. Her hair was blue fire eating at her scalp, fed by the slender life of her body.

Four days had passed and still she was young . . . no, younger, than when they had entered the ship. She was still adolescent.

He could not believe it.

Her first words were, "How long will this last?"

He replied, carefully, "I don't know."

"We are still young."

"The ship. Its metal is around us. It cuts away the sun and the things that came from the sun to age us."

Her eyes shifted thoughtfully. "Then, if we stay here—"

"We'll remain young."

"Six more days? Fourteen more? Twenty?"

"More than that, maybe."

She lay there, silently. After a long time she said, "Sim?"

"Yes."

"Let's stay here. Let's not go back. If we go back now,

you know what'll happen to us . . . ?"

"I'm not certain."

"We'll start getting old again, won't we?"

He looked away. He stared at the ceiling and the clock with the moving finger. "Yes. We'll grow old."

"What if we grow old—instantly. When we step from the ship won't the shock be too much?"

"Maybe."

Another silence. He began to move his limbs, testing them. He was very hungry. "The others are waiting," he said.

Her next words made him gasp. "The others are dead," she said. "Or will be in a few hours. All those we knew back there are old."

He tried to picture them old. Dark, his sister, bent and senile with time. He shook his head, wiping the picture away. "They may die," he said. "But there are others who've been born."

"People we don't even know."

"But, nevertheless, *our* people," he replied. "People who'll live only eight days, or eleven days unless we help them."

"But we're *young*, Sim! We can *stay* young!"

He didn't want to listen. It was too tempting a thing to listen to. To stay here. To live. "We've already had more time than the others," he said. "I need workers. Men to heal this ship. We'll get on our feet now, you and I, and find food, eat, and see if the ship is movable. I'm afraid to try to move it myself. It's so big. I'll need help."

"But that means running back all that distance!"

"I know." He lifted himself weakly. "But I'll do it."

"How will you get the men back here?"

"We'll use the river."

"*If* it's there. It *may* be somewhere else."

"We'll wait until there *is* one, then. I've got to go back, Lyte. The son of Dienc is waiting for me, my sister, your brother, are old people, ready to die, and waiting for some word from us—"

After a long while he heard her move, dragging herself tiredly to him. She put her head upon his chest, her eyes closed, stroking his arm. "I'm sorry. Forgive me. You have to go back. I'm a selfish fool."

He touched her cheek, clumsily. "You're human. I understand you. There's nothing to forgive."

They found food. They walked through the ship. It was empty. Only in the control room did they find the remains of a man who must have been the chief pilot. The others had evidently bailed out into space in emergency lifeboats. This pilot, sitting at his controls, alone, had landed the ship on a mountain within sight of other fallen and smashed crafts. Its location on high ground had saved it from the floods. The pilot himself had died, probably of heart failure, soon after landing. The ship had remained here, almost within reach of the other survivors, perfect as an egg, but silent, for—how many thousand days? If the pilot had lived, what a different thing life might have been for the ancestors of Sim and Lyte. Sim, thinking of this, felt the distant, ominous vibration of war. How had the war between worlds come out? Who had won? Or had both planets lost and never bothered trying to pick up survivors? Who had been right? Who was the enemy? Were Sim's people of the guilty or innocent side? They might never know.

He checked the ship hurriedly. He knew nothing of its workings, yet as he walked its corridors, patted its machines, he learned from it. It needed only a crew. One man couldn't possibly set the whole thing running again. He laid his hand upon one round, snoutlike machine. He jerked his hand away, as if burnt.

"Lyte!"

"What is it?"

He touched the machine again, caressed it, his hand trembled violently, his eyes welled with tears, his mouth opened and closed, he looked at the machine, loving it, then looked at Lyte.

"With this machine—" he stammered, softly, incredulously. "With— With this machine I can—"

"What, Sim?"

He inserted his hand into a cuplike contraption with a lever inside. Out of the porthole in front of him he could see the distant line of cliffs. "We were afraid there might never be another river running by this mountain, weren't we?" he asked, exultantly.

"Yes, Sim, but—"

"There *will* be a river. And I *will* come back, tonight! and I'll bring men with me. Five hundred men! Because with this machine I can blast a river bottom all the way to the cliffs, down which the waters will rush, giving myself and the men a swift, sure way of traveling back!" He rubbed the machine's barrellike body. "When I touched it, the life and method of it burnt into me! Watch!" He depressed the lever.

A beam of incandescent fire lanced out from the ship, screaming.

Steadily, accurately, Sim began to cut away a riverbed for the storm waters to flow in. The night was turned to day by its hungry eating.

* * *

The return to the cliffs was to be carried out by Sim alone. Lyte was to remain in the ship, in case of any mishap. The trip back seemed, at first glance, to be impossible. There would be no river rushing to cut his time, to sweep him along toward his destination. He would have to run the entire distance in the dawn, and the sun would get him, catch him before he'd reached safety.

"The only way to do it is to start *before* sunrise."

"But you'd be frozen, Sim."

"Here." He made adjustments on the machine that had just finished cutting the riverbed in the rock floor of the valley. He lifted the smooth snout of the gun, pressed the lever, left it down. A gout of fire shot toward the cliffs. He fingered the range control, focused the flame end three miles from its source. Done. He turned to Lyte. "But I don't understand," she said.

He opened the air-lock door. "It's bitter cold out, and half an hour yet till dawn. If I run parallel to the flame from the machine, close enough to it, there'll not be much heat, but enough to sustain life, anyway."

"It doesn't sound safe," Lyte protested.

"Nothing does, on this world." He moved forward. "I'll have a half-hour start. That should be enough to reach the cliffs."

"But if the machine should fail while you're still running near its beam?"

"Let's not think of that," he said.

A moment later he was outside. He staggered as if kicked in the stomach. His heart almost exploded in him. The environment of his world forced him into swift living again. He felt his pulse rise, kicking through his veins.

The night was cold as death. The heat ray from the ship sliced across the valley, humming, solid and warm. He moved next to it, very close. One misstep in his running and—

"I'll be back," he called to Lyte.

He and the ray of light went together.

In the early morning the people in the caves saw the long finger of orange incandescence and the weird whitish apparition floating, running along beside it. There was muttering and moaning and many sighs of awe.

And when Sim finally reached the cliffs of his childhood he saw alien peoples swarming there. There were no familiar faces. Then he realized how foolish it was to expect familiar faces. One of the older men glared down at him: "Who're you?" he shouted. "Are you from the enemy cliff? What's your name?"

"Lam Sim, the son of Sim!"

"Sim!"

An old woman shrieked from the cliff above him. She came hobbling down the stone pathway. "Sim, Sim, it *is* you!"

He looked at her frankly bewildered. "But I don't know you," he murmured.

"Sim, don't you recognize me? Oh, Sim, it's me! Dark!"

"Dark!"

He felt sick at his stomach. She fell into his arms. This old trembling woman with the half-blind eyes, his sister.

Another face appeared above. That of an old man. A cruel, bitter face. It looked down at Sim and snarled. "Drive him away!" cried the old man. "He comes from the cliff of the enemy. He's lived there! He's still young! Those who go there can never come back among us. Disloyal beast!" And a rock hurtled down.

Sim leaped aside, pulling the old woman with him.

A roar came from the people. They ran toward Sim, shaking their fists. "Kill him, kill him!" raved the old man, and Sim did not know who he was.

"Stop!" Sim held out his hands. "I come from the ship!"

"The ship?" The people slowed. Dark clung to him, looking up into his young face, puzzling over its smoothness.

"Kill him, kill him, kill him!" croaked the old man, and picked up another rock.

"I offer you ten days, twenty days, thirty more days of life!"

The people stopped. Their mouths hung open. Their eyes were incredulous.

"Thirty days?" It was repeated again and again. "How?"

"Come back to the ship with me. Inside it, one can live forever!"

The old man lifted high a rock, then, choking, fell forward in an apoplectic fit, and tumbled down the rocks to lie at Sim's feet.

Sim bent to peer at the ancient one, at the raw, dead eyes, the loose, sneering lips, the crumpled, quiet body.

"Chion!"

"Yes," said Dark behind him, in a croaking, strange voice. "Your enemy. Chion."

That night two hundred men started for the ship. The water ran in the new channel. One hundred of them were drowned or lost behind in the cold. The others, with Sim, got through to the ship.

Lyte awaited them, and threw wide the metal door.

The weeks passed. Generations lived and died in the cliffs, while the scientists and workers labored over the ship, learning its functions and its parts.

On the last day, two dozen men moved to their stations within the ship. Now there was a destiny of travel ahead.

Sim touched the control plates under his fingers.

Lyte, rubbing her eyes, came and sat on the floor next to him, resting her head against his knee, drowsily. "I had a dream," she said, looking off at something far away. "I dreamed I lived in caves in a cliff on a cold-hot planet where people grew old and died in eight days."

"What an impossible dream," said Sim. "People couldn't possibly live in such a nightmare. Forget it. You're awake now."

He touched the plates gently. The ship rose and moved into space.

Sim was right.

The nightmare was over at last.

Guys Read sci-fi and fantasy stuff. And you just proved it. (Unless you just opened the book to this page and started reading. In which case, we feel bad for you because you missed some pretty awesome stuff.)

Now what?

Now we keep going—Guys Read keeps working to find good stuff for you to read, you read it and pass it along to other guys. Here's how we can do it.

For ten years, Guys Read has been at www.guysread.com, collecting recommendations of what guys really want to read. We have gathered recommendations of thousands of great funny books, scary books, action books, illustrated books, information books, wordless books, sci-fi books, mystery books, and you-name-it books.

So what's your part of the job? Simple: try out some of the suggestions at guysread.com, try some of the other stuff written by the authors in this book, then let us know what you think. Tell us what you like to read. Tell us what you don't like to read. The more you tell us, the more great book recommendations we can collect. It might even help us choose the writers for the next installment of Guys Read.

Thanks for reading.

And thanks for helping Guys Read.

JON SCIESZKA (editor) has been writing books for children ever since he took time off from his career as an elementary school teacher. He wanted to create funny books that kids would want to read. Once he got going, he never stopped. He is the author of numerous picture books, middle grade series, and even a memoir. From 2007–2010 he served as the first National Ambassador for Children's Literature, appointed by the Library of Congress. Since 2004, Jon has been actively promoting his interest in getting boys to read through his Guys Read initiative and website. Born in Flint, Michigan, Jon now lives in Brooklyn with his family. Visit him online at www.jsworldwide.com and at www.guysread.com.

SELECTED TITLES

THE TRUE STORY OF THE THREE LITTLE PIGS
(Illustrated by Lane Smith)

THE STINKY CHEESE MAN
AND OTHER FAIRLY STUPID TALES
(Illustrated by Lane Smith)

The Time Warp Trio series, including SUMMER READING
IS KILLING ME (Illustrated by Lane Smith)

The Spaceheadz series

TOM ANGLEBERGER ("Rise of the RoboShoes™") began writing his first novel in eighth grade, but never completed it. Since then, he's been a newspaper reporter and columnist, a juggler, a weed boy, a lawn-mower-part assembler, and a biology research assistant. This bestselling author insists he's not really all that creative—"I'm more of a puzzle-putter-together." You can visit him online at www.origamiyoda.wordpress.com.

SELECTED TITLES

The Origami Yoda series, including THE STRANGE CASE OF ORIGAMI YODA

HORTON HALFPOTT

FAKE MUSTACHE

When he was twelve years old, **RAY BRADBURY** ("Frost and Fire") met a carnival magician, Mr. Electrico, who touched him with his sword and commanded: "Live forever!" Ray later said, "I decided that was the greatest idea I had ever heard." He immediately began writing every day, and continued to do so for the rest of his life—nearly seventy years—writing hundreds of short stories and close to fifty books.

SELECTED TITLES

DANDELION WINE

THE ILLUSTRATED MAN

THE MARTIAN CHRONICLES

SHANNON HALE ("Bouncing the Grinning Goat") began writing at age ten—mostly fantasy stories where she was the heroine. She never stopped. She writes bestselling books for kids and adults and also writes graphic novels. Her book PRINCESS ACADEMY was named a Newbery Honor Book in 2006. Shannon lives with her family near Salt Lake City, Utah. You can visit her online at www.squeetus.com.

SELECTED TITLES
The Books of Bayern, including THE GOOSE GIRL

BOOK OF A THOUSAND DAYS

CALAMITY JACK
(With Dean Hale, illustrated by Nathan Hale)

D. J. MACHALE ("The Scout") is a bestselling author and is also a director, executive producer, and creator of several popular television series and movies. He lives in Southern California with his family, where they spend a lot of time backpacking, scuba diving, and skiing. You can visit him online at www.djmachalebooks.com.

SELECTED TITLES
The Pendragon series,
including THE MERCHANT OF DEATH
The Morpheus Road trilogy, including THE LIGHT
The SYLO trilogy, including SYLO

ERIC NYLUND ("The Warlords of Recess") is a *New York Times* bestselling and World Fantasy Award–nominated author of fourteen published science fiction, fantasy, and YA novels. His latest is a science fiction series for young readers, The Resisters. Eric also works for Microsoft Studios, where he makes video games.

SELECTED TITLES

The Resistors series, including TITAN BASE

The Mortal Coils series, including
ALL THAT LIVES MUST DIE

The Halo series, including THE FALL OF REACH

KENNETH OPPEL ("The Klack Bros. Museum") got his first encouragement as a writer when a story he wrote at age fourteen made its way to Roald Dahl, who in turn sent it to his own agent, who took Ken on as a client. Since then, Ken has written many award-winning and bestselling books. He lives with his family in Toronto. You can find him online at www.kennethoppel.ca.

SELECTED TITLES

AIRBORN

SILVERWING

THIS DARK ENDEAVOR:
The Apprenticeship of Victor Frankenstein

RICK RIORDAN ("Percy Jackson and the Singer of Apollo")
is a bestselling author of adventure books for kids and mysteries for adults. Rick is also a former middle school teacher
who taught mythology every year. You can visit him online
at www.rickriordan.com.

SELECTED TITLES

Percy Jackson and the Olympians series, including
THE LIGHTNING THIEF

Heroes of Olympus series, including THE LOST HERO

The Kane Chronicles series, including THE RED PYRAMID

NEAL SHUSTERMAN ("The Dirt on Our Shoes") grew up
in Brooklyn, New York, where he began writing at an early
age. He has been successful as a novelist for both kids and
adults, as a screenwriter, and as a television writer. He has
also directed two short films. You can visit him online at
www.storyman.com.

SELECTED TITLES

The Skinjacker Trilogy, including EVERLOST

UNWIND

THE SCHWA WAS HERE

REBECCA STEAD ("Plan B") went to the kind of elementary school where a person could sit on a windowsill or even under a table to read a book, and no one told you to come out and be serious. After trying to be serious as a lawyer for a while, she decided to be a full-time writer. Her book WHEN YOU REACH ME was awarded the Newbery Medal in 2010 and was a *New York Times* bestseller. She lives in New York City with her family. You can visit her online at www.rebeccasteadbooks.com.

SELECTED TITLES

FIRST LIGHT

WHEN YOU REACH ME

LIAR & SPY

SHAUN TAN ("A Day in the Life") grew up in Perth, Western Australia, and made up for the fact that he was the shortest kid in every class by being known as a "good drawer." Besides working full-time as an illustrator of his own stories, Shaun has worked as a designer in theater and film, and also directed the Academy Award–winning short film *The Lost Thing*. You can visit him online at www.shauntan.net.

SELECTED TITLES

THE ARRIVAL

TALES FROM OUTER SUBURBIA

THE RED TREE

GREG RUTH (Illustrator) has created countless comic books for Dark Horse and other publishers, and has worked on videos for Prince and Rob Thomas, among others. He has also illustrated many children's books as well as graphic novels. He lives with his family in Massachusetts.

SELECTED TITLES

FREAKS OF THE HEARTLAND
(Written by Steve Niles)

CONAN: BORN ON THE BATTLEFIELD
(Written by Kurt Busiek)

The Secret Journeys of Jack London series,
including THE WILD
(Written by Christopher Golden and Tim Lebbon)